SIGNIFICANT OTHERS

Love and death in Cyprus

Glenis K.Scadding

ISBN: 9798426216631

Imprint: Independently published

Cover photograph by: Glenis Scadding

Dedicated to my aunts- all of them.

There is only one happiness in this life, to love and be loved. George Sand.

SIGNIFICANT OTHERS

CHAPTER 1

Now it is my favourite wedding photo. Then it was a disaster.

In it the bride, framed with her handsome new husband in the ancient church porch, looks aghast: glassy eyed, mouth dropped, hands flung wide, bouquet tumbling.

Immediately after it was taken I subsided gracefully to the stone floor, squashing that expensive floral display. The photographer backed off. The congregation, unaware of events, continued singing lustily, asking the King of Heaven to Praise their Souls. My new spouse knelt beside me, calling my name, and stroking my face. The cause of the commotion turned and fled through the graveyard.

My mother- having been urgently summoned by my maid of honour- reached me whilst I was still

pale and sweating, on the ground.

"My darling, whatever happened?"

"I saw her."

"Who?"

"Ti."

My mother said nothing, just bent down and hugged me. After a minute she whispered in my ear.

"Probably because you really wanted her to be here. Come on now, Upsidaisy Whoa."

I nodded, reassured by the childhood terminology, and began to rise, helped by Mum and Nick.

In subsequent photos if you look carefully, you can see dust marks on the dress and a distant strained

expression on my face. My maid of honour kindly lent me her bouquet for the remainder of the day-

it was that which I sent flying over my shoulder before departing with Nick for our honeymoon.

A recent pre- nuptial trip up to the attic, via the wobbly expanding ladder, to look for Mum's

wedding headdress (something borrowed) had unnerved me. Life- size cardboard cut- out figures lay along the front wall, looking uncomfortable and unloved, stiffly held by sticks attached to their undersides. One time there had been a very big cardboard box from the new fridge freezer and Ti had turned it into a puppet theatre. We did shows, all of which were compulsory viewing for Mum and Dad when they came home. They made appreciative noises, aided in part by the accompanying G&T.

Eventually the theatre had begun to fold.

The memory was vivid.

"It's breaking, Ti!"

"Where?"

"Here- and here." I pointed to the long split down one side, and a shorter one down another.

"Never mind sweetheart. Time for a change."

"What are we going to do?"

"We are going to make art sweetheart. Life-size art project starting now."

Ti took the breadknife to the split and sawed it open it all the way done, then freed up the other sides of the box. There were four large pieces of cardboard.

"Lie on this one and I'll draw round you."

The three of us obliged, then we drew round Ti on the last piece.

"Get the poster paints please, Chloe"

We each painted ourselves wearing the clothes we were in, then when Ti drew herself in an evening

gown with a tiara we followed suit and jazzed up our icons. When dry we stuck them onto the

bamboo sticks that were usually reserved for the runner beans and set them up in the garden.

Oscar, our silly dog, barked and barked at them so much that the neighbours complained- so they

were brought indoors and found their way to the attic, joining boxes of other stuff made by me at

school and brought home for approbation.

The life-size figures, propped along the side wall, stared at me, bringing memories and unease.

Dorian Gray in reverse, I thought. Where are you now, Ti?

CHAPTER 2

As soon as we were alone together in the car, I asked Nick if he had noticed anything as we

emerged from the church. He thought for a moment, brow wrinkling little, before saying,

"Yes, there was someone, a woman, watching from behind one of the

bigger gravestones, off to the side. Just as I noticed her you swooned, that's the word for it,

swooned, so I didn't see her again. No idea who she was, or even how old she was, it was just a

glimpse."

The relief was enormous.

"Oh, thank goodness. Mum thought I'd imagined it. I wondered if I was going mad."

"Now is a great time to tell me that Mrs. Nicolaou!" He turned towards me, making a moue face.

"Keep your eyes on the road, Mr Rochester."

"Oh, very funny. Who was she anyway?"

"My aunt, Ti, I think.

"Your auntie?" Nick was surprised at my choice of word.

"No", I laughed," not my auntie but my aunt Ti. Ti is what I called her. Short for Felicity."

"Called?" he picked up the past tense. I knew why I loved him- or one of the reasons anyway, he was so quick on the uptake.

 "Ti is dead."

"Goodness! Tell me about it."

You may think it strange that Nick did not know about Ti. It was odd- I had met him after her

death and had not wanted to talk about her. The hurt was such that I compartmentalized it and

rarely opened that box. My parents knew better than to discuss Ti with me as it merely provoked

tears.

So for Nick it was as though she had not existed, yet she was there in my memories.

Walking home from school with Ti in charge, playing I-spy with us, then chasing us as "it."

"Your Mum is much more fun than mine," Becky complained.

"She's not my Mum. Ti is my aunt, my Mum's sister. She just lives with us."

"Why?"

"Her Mum and Dad are abroad. Ti was at boarding school, but now she's not."

"Why?"

"Dunno, come on I'll race you to the gate."

In my eagerness to win I pushed back too hard with my right foot, gravel on the path slid beneath it and I went face down whump onto the pavement. For a brief moment I was shocked into silence, then I felt the hurt on my knee and I began to wail.

"Upsadaisy Whoa! Chloe, upsadaisy whoa. Let me have a look at your leg, sweetheart." Ti had a hand on my back, steadying me, she circled it gently round, soothing my distress.

"There's a brave girl. Here, dry your tears."

A tissue found its way into my hands. I held it to my eyes and then snorted into it.

Becky laughed.

"Oh Becky, don't be mean. I bet you'd have made even more fuss!" Ti admonished her.

"Now, I happen to know that there is homemade lemonade for tea. Who wants some?"

Did you make it Ti?

"No, your Mum did. She was at home all day today, just for once."

CHAPTER 3

As we drove to the airport hotel, I began to explain.

"Ti was my mother's younger sister. She was closer in age to me, since the age gap between

her and my mother was 13 years and Ti was only 12 when I was born. Apparently, Ti was over the

moon to have a niece- and spent lots of time with me that first summer. Her parents, my maternal

grandparents, were stationed overseas- so Ti was at a boarding school, Cheltenham Ladies College,

in England. My mother, after difficult pregnancy and a Caesarean, was finding life hard. She was

only too happy for Ti to come each weekend, wheel me out in the pram, round the park, to the

shops and for Ti to learn how to feed me with a bottle, change my nappy, sing me to sleep. I must have been like a real -life dolly. Ti and I bonded in a way that my mother and I have never really

managed. With hindsight I think Mum had postnatal depression and also that I was a mistake. Both

she and Dad are very career- orientated and suffer badly from the Protestant work ethic. Having a

family probably had not featured in their plans for the future."

Nick nodded. I continued.

"Ti had to leave Cheltenham, where she'd been unhappy and had been caught smoking dope. There

wasn't a suitable English school in Slovenia where Gran and Grandpa were- so Mum agreed to take

her in so Ti could go to a London day school- but it was also for her babysitting potential, I suspect.

 I was about two at the time. Ti would give me my tea, play with me, sometimes she would have to

put me to bed and read to me. I loved having her there and missed her when she went away some holidays and weekends. "Upsadaisy Whoa" was what Ti said when I was little and fell over or hurt

myself. Later it was used for other hurts, like falling out with a friend or doing badly in a test. It

became a family word meaning "get up and get on with it."

A pause while I went over the last time I'd heard that phrase. Had I seen a ghost?

"Go on my love," said Nick.

"Things began to go wrong when I was five and Ti was doing her A- levels, had a boyfriend and had

less time for me. I was hurt and not inclined to be generous enough to allow her time to study, so

she began to stay over at friends' houses. The au pair was asked to do longer hours; I treated her so

badly because she wasn't Ti that she left. My Mum was very cross, my Dad too. They told me that I

was selfish and unkind and sent me to bed early with no story. Once my tears had dried, I decided to run away, find Ti and live with her. My memory is hazy, but I managed to leave the house and enter

the nearby park, which was still open because it was summer and still light.

It was still warm, and the air smelled of hay and dust. I wandered in my pyjamas between families picnicking on the grass, heading for the swings. Nobody stopped me until, unable to find Ti and with very itchy eyes, I began to sniffle.

A voice came to interrupt what had become my wailing.

"Hello, what's wrong? Are you lost?"

I looked up. My wet eyes could hardly see him, but it was a man speaking and smiling too.

I nodded.

"Can I take you home?"

More nodding.

"Do you know your address?"

Proudly I spouted it, having been taught by Ti from an early age, just in case.

"Oh that's near where I live. We can go together. It's this way."

He held out his hand and I took it confidently with a child's perception of goodness.

On the way he carried on talking to me.

"My name is Kostas. What's your name?"

"Chloe."

"Khloe, oh that's a Greek name. Do you know what it means?"

I shook my head.

"It means a young plant which is growing. What a lovely name to have. My name is Greek too. I am Greek from Cyprus. My family live in the Greek part of the island."

Kostas- or Costas as he spelt it in England – carried on chatting reassuringly as we walked. I held his big warm hand tightly and was a little sad when we reached my house.

My father's face when he answered the door was a moving picture of astonishment, alarm, then relief. My discoverer was invited in to be thanked with a drink, I was put back into bed, with

antihistamine and admonitions. My parents, once they realized that Costas was not a child molester,

took to him and continued to see him from time to time while he studied in London.

"Ti's A- level results were not up to expectations. She may have blamed me, I don't know. At the

time I had no feelings of guilt and she never said anything to me. The expectation was that she

would go to university and qualify as some kind of professional- but Ti refused to live out others'

dreams, at least that is what she said."

"Sweetheart I don't want to end up like your Mum, nor mine. Where is the magic in their lives?"

I thought she had a point, though I'd have liked to be thought of as magic in Mum's life.

"What will you do then?"

"Tell no- one, but I have a plan. I am going to become a singer."

"On the TV?"

"Maybe one day, if I am lucky. But for now I've got bookings in pubs and clubs with my mates,

Tommy and Kemal. We've formed a group. Guess what we're called?"

My knowledge of the pop music scene was minimal. In our house classical music held sway. I knew

one name only, that of the Beatles.

"Umm, the Earwigs?"

Ti was kind enough not to snort with laughter.

"Good one, but no- we're the Ti-Pots."

My face must have been a puzzle.

"It's from my nickname, Ti and pot", she explained.

I was no nearer. I thought it a very silly name.

CHAPTER 4

Ti came and went, sometimes she was elated at the group's success, sometimes quiet when things

weren't going well. The quiet times became more frequent. I overheard my Mum talking to Ti in the kitchen one day. I was eight or nine, off school, supposed to

be upstairs in bed with an asthma attack, but had crept down because I'd heard Ti's voice and

wanted to see her.

"You treat this place like a hotel. You appear when it suits you, stay for as long as you see fit and

then just disappear, without a word."

"I'm so sorry. I don't mean to take you for granted. You know I love seeing you all, especially Chloe. I

don't always know when I'm going to be back in London- or I'd let you know. Do you want me to

stop coming?"

There was a pause. I held my breath. Don't say yes Mum, don't say yes. Fortunately, I didn't need to say it aloud.

"No, of course not, we love having you here. I'd appreciate more notice of your movements, that's

all. There will always be a home for you with us" she corrected herself, "with me."

"How are things with David?"

No words came but I could see my Mum shaking her head, hunching her shoulders. Ti put her arms

around her. I crept back to bed.

Other memories were more cheerful- Ti taking me to the cinema, the theatre, the Zoo. She was "fun

to be with": time together was always fun. She added much- needed colour to my dull routine life.

She also added a little wickedness from time to time: my first cigarette, then the initial taste of pot,

were with her. Fortunately, both made me cough and choke, so I found them not worth repeating.

A few years ago, Ti and I were playing boules one day in the park. She had encouraged me out of the

house where I'd been miserably studying. I sent a ball which was unexpectedly successful in

knocking two of hers away from the target.

"Hey, Chloe the destroyer! Good shot! You've done it again"

"What? No, I've never managed that before."

"Oh yes you did. Simply by arriving on the scene."

"What?"

"Before you turned up your Mum and Dad were on track to hit their targets."

"That's a mean thing to say."

"Chlo, it's not your fault, but it explains so much. You need to know. It's why you and your Mum find

it hard to get on with each other."

"Tell me what you mean then."

"Kate met David at Uni. She says it was love at first sight and they got engaged in a few months.

Neither family was pleased though. Kate and I come from a staunch Catholic family; David's ancestry

was Protestant Huguenot, which is where your de Sanges surname comes from."

I nodded, having been aware of this since a small child because when we stayed with Gran and

Grandad de Sanges, we went to a big church where Mum and Dad received bread (well wafers) as

well as wine. Grandad got all dressed up and stood at the front, praying or speaking to us. Only later

did I realise that he was the Bishop.

"Well Kate and I have been brought up to regard contraception as a sin. You do know what I mean

by contraception?"

"Yes, we've done reproduction at school."

"So, the rhythm method failed, and you arrived 10 months after the wedding."

"And I was not welcome?"

"You were earlier than they'd wanted. They had little time to enjoy being a young married couple,

too little time to get established in their careers and they were a bit scared too. A baby is a big

responsibility and a lot of work. They love you dearly, but you pushed them apart. David blamed

Kate, she got depressed, found it hard to cope. "

"I thought babies brought people together."

"Sometimes, I guess; sometimes not. You were often ill and that made things worse. Hurried trips to

hospital, sleeping there in a chair, worn out at work, Kate lost a good job for poor attendance. She

blamed David because he was not around to help. He withdrew, works all week, golfs most of the

weekend."

It made sense of something that I had half realised.

"So that's why Mum is often cross with me over nothing?"

Ti nodded.

"She's not depressed anymore and she's worked her way back into a worthwhile job, but I don't

think she has many real friends. She's lonely and with Mum and Dad abroad I'm her only family

support. I am telling you this Chlo because I see you being sad and think it's time you knew that

none of it is your fault."

It had made me feel better to know why I was often less than happy. Going to Uni was a surprisingly

wonderful experience for me- I made good friends early on with seriously kind people. To be among

friends who cared about what I felt and thought, without having to return each night to the sterile

environment of my home, was enlivening. COVID-19 destroyed that, leaving me stuck with my

parents. No wonder I was keen to emerge from lockdown. Surprisingly they had adapted to it well:

forced to spend time together they had grated off their encrustations, rediscovered their mutual

interests. In the mornings they attacked the crossword, lunch time was spent in the garden, in the

evenings they would watch old films. Dad called Mum "Kate" more often now, instead of Katherine.

She occasionally used "Dave", though it did not suit my buttoned -up Dad. I began to understand

what they had meant to each other and felt excluded from their re- alliance. No wonder that I had

been glad to meet Nick.

CHAPTER 5

"Please may I buy you a drink?"

I swivelled on my bar stool to see where the voice came from. It was emanating from the rather

beautiful mouth of an undeniably handsome, dark- haired young man. He looked like James Norton,

only younger. My heart leapt- it really felt as though it had moved up to my mouth- making me

almost gasp. I turned it into a smile.

"Oh, no, thank you. My friend is coming soon."

I had been so keen to get out once the lockdown was over that I'd arrived uncharacteristically early

at the Jewel Bar.

"OK, but I'm happy to give you a drink while you wait- no strings," he replied. "It's just so good to be

out again. I feel the need to celebrate."

"Me too. In that case I'd like a Coke please." There was no way I was going to allow him to buy me

one of the delicious sounding, but expensive, cocktails.

"Coming up." He caught the barmaid's eye and ordered my drink plus a Negroni for himself.

"Do you live near here?" His eyes were brown and deep. He looked older than me or my friends.

"No, I've braved the Tube to get here, masked up, of course." I found myself gabbling. "There's a

small group of us meeting here to celebrate the end of our Uni. Courses. It's a big let-down because

we've been learning from home since mid-March and there are no final exams, no graduation

ceremony- so we thought we'd do something to mark the occasion."

The drinks arrived- he handed me my glass, clinked it with his and said,

"Cheers! To your degree."

We drank. I had forgotten how gassy Coke was and regretted the big slurp as soon as it hit my throat

and began to go down the wrong way.

I began to cough.

"Steady now." He patted my back gently at first, then more firmly, until the coughing ceased and I,

red- faced with embarrassment, could breathe and speak again.

"Sorry."

"No need to apologize. It happens to everyone sometime. What was the nature of your degree?"

Here came the T- test as I call it.

"Theology."

That is a chat- down word. However, it rapidly achieves sheep/ goat sorting, which makes it useful.

Those who respond with

"Are you going to be some sort of vicar?"

Or "Whatever for?"

Or even "WTF is that?" are non – starters in the race to win my heart. Not that there are many

 starters.

"That is most interesting. Did it include all the major religions?"

The dark handsome stranger with his formal language had passed the test.

I was beginning to explain the fascinating content of the Theology course, ranging from miracles, to

the death of the Buddha to ethics and religion etc., when Angie arrived, closely followed by David and Karl. We greeted each other with the requisite elbow bumps- no hugs, no kisses allowed. I

started to introduce the young man- but realised that I did not know his name.

"Good evening, I am Nicholas Nicolaou, known as Nick" he said, "I was looking after this young lady

until you arrived."

He looked at me quizzically.

"Chloe," I said, offering my elbow.

"Enchanted to meet you, Chloe. I would be interested to hear more about your theology course

sometime, would that be possible?"

"Sure- here's my phone number." I scribbled it onto a napkin, hoping that it would not run or fade

before he tried to use it.

My group moved off to claim their table. I went to join them, then glanced back, but Nick was

gone.

"Wow, you pulled well there," Angie sounded a mite jealous.

"Hope so," I replied. The idea of love at first sight had always seemed ridiculous to me, but I must admit that I was already smitten.

It was the next day that Nick rang and invited me out. He was obviously as keen as I was.

We braved a restaurant- a quiet, ethnic one not far from my home. Nick got on famously with the

waiter who turned out to be the son of the proprietor. He was doing the cooking, but emerged to

chat to us, initially in English, then to Nick in Greek. He gave us a wonderful house salad, including

coriander, which I love, followed by the best kebabs I have ever tasted. We sat outside and

talked and talked and talked. Mostly about me, now that I think of it. Having spent weeks at home

locked down with my parents it was a relief to speak to someone of my generation in the flesh, not

just by phone or computer and I poured out my heart to him. Nick was more circumspect. I learnt

that he was a businessman involved in import/ export, no specific items mentioned, and that he

lived with friends in Reading. He'd been in the Jewel Bar the evening before to meet a possible

business contact, but the bloke had failed to turn up. Nick had been about to leave when he saw me sitting alone and decided to speak to me.

"I'm glad you did."

CHAPTER 6

"We have arrived," Nick announced as the car turned into the driveway of a smallish hotel on the outskirts of Gatwick.

I was glad that it was not one of the amorphous chain hotels that you find inside airports and said so.

"So far, so good." I said.

"I thought you would prefer something like this."

When you have just married someone, you haven't known that long it is very reassuring when they get things right about you.

"Will you tell me now where we're going for our honeymoon?"

My fingers were mentally crossed that it would be somewhere I'd like. Not that it really matters I

told myself- one couple of my parents' vintage survived the awful realisation that the walking trip

along Hadrian's Wall was not what the bride would have chosen- not even in her wildest dreams.

Their silver wedding was enlivened by the story told from both sides.

"Tomorrow," Nick promised.

That evening he borrowed my passport in order to check us in and had the boarding passes printed

by the hotel, keeping them hidden from me.

Our honeymoon night was, I suspect, like many others undertaken by tired couples who have been through a church service, greeted many friends, overeaten, travelled, then had to set the alarm clock for an early hour. Remarkable it was not.

The next morning Nick had made me a cup of coffee before waking me. That augured well. We dressed hurriedly and caught the transport to the airport terminal.

"North or South?" I asked, still with no idea of our destination, other than the fact that it would be warm in mid- September.

"They are still only using the North terminal because flights are much fewer since COVID."

"Oh, was it hard to get a flight to wherever we are going?"

"The choice was limited. I think you will like it, though. I hope so."

Once through security he steered me towards one of the high numbered departure gates. When we reached it the destination read Larnaca.

"Larnaca, that's Cyprus, isn't it? Was that why we had to have COVID tests?"

Nick nodded.

"Is Cyprus what you wanted?" he asked

I hesitated, wanting to please him, but having my own thoughts to work through. I was polite.

"Yes, thank you. I'm sure it will be lovely."

It was strange – I had half-expected, half-wanted to go there anyway.

"You do not sound sure. Have I done the wrong thing?"

"No, no, not at all. It's just odd, having thought I saw Ti yesterday. You see Cyprus is where she died."

"Oh, I am very sorry. I did not know of this. Will you be all right?"

"Yes."

I couldn't say more, I was too overwhelmed by the memory of those final days of Ti's life and by my

failure to speak to her before it ended. The regret was huge. The garbled, uninterpretable message

on my phone- which I had discovered as a missed call late one night in the UK. Cyprus was 2 hours

ahead, so I had not returned it immediately, but had left it for the morning, even though Mum had

told me that Ti had COVID-19.

When I rang the number back next day it was answered by a stranger who asked who I was, then

kindly and gently told me that Ti had died in the night. You know that Superman film where he turns

back the clock so he can do the right thing- that is what I have wanted to do ever since. I'd given

Mum's name as next of kin and she had taken over from there. I mentally walked away from all of it.

There was a boarding call, so I was forced to switch my attention to the real world and get into line.

Nick had paid for Club class tickets to give us space since COVID -19 was still not completely

controlled. The vaccine shots we'd received earlier in 2021 were not guaranteed to protect us for

more than 6 months and it was now mid- September. We boarded quickly and spent time setting

ourselves up in our spacious leather front seats. Once the cases had been safely stowed, papers,

magazines and books shoved into pockets and a glass of Buck's Fizz accepted for the sake of

politeness, we were free to talk again.

Nick explained that he loved Cyprus. He'd been there often as a child because his paternal

grandparents were Greek Cypriots and he wanted to introduce me to places he knew. No people

though, his antecedents were now sadly dead and he had no close relatives left.

"Would you like to tell me more about Ti?" Nick was solicitous. "It might help."

He was right. I had bottled up my feelings of sadness and guilt for too long- so as we taxied slowly,

queued for take- off and then rumbled faster and faster down the runway I unburdened myself,

stopping only for the exciting moments when the surly bonds of terra firma are left behind and then

there is that hesitant pause when the engines stop being at full throttle, leaving the impression that

a sudden swoop back down might conceivably happen. Then I went on.

"Ti was in Cyprus because she had got married there in Spring 2019. It was all pretty sudden- she'd

met this man on a cruise ship where she was singing. The boat had started from Australia and was

making its way, via every place you can think of, to Southampton. As usual the internet on board was lousy so few messages were sent. According to what Ti told Mum later, it was a shipboard romance

which became serious, so much so that when they reached Limassol, the Cyprus port, they

abandoned ship and went to his house. They were married as soon as possible- so quickly that there

was no time to invite family over. Though it was not openly discussed we all privately thought Ti was

pregnant. We received some wedding photos by e – mail, then eventually desiccated wedding cake pieces by snail mail.

We were not totally surprised: Ti had always been somewhat unpredictable. I felt hurt that I had not

been in her confidence- but glad that she had finally settled down. Andrei sounded nice- and was

apparently seriously rich. He'd bought a beautiful property at Sea Caves, north of Paphos. It faced

west – "so he could watch the sunsets, but the purchase also meant that he could obtain Cyprus citizenship."

No news was, we hoped, good news. Mum tried her on WhatsApp each week, the replies were

sparse, but enthusiastic, with lots of exclamation marks and abundant love to us all.

"Cyprus is sooo beautiful. You must come and stay."

She texted this to me and I replied affirming my desire to see both her and Cyprus- but no actual

definite plan or dates emerged. Then came the coronavirus. Ti rang Mum when we were in

lockdown to let her know that she had the illness but was fine. Andrei was not; being older and

male it had affected him badly and he was in hospital. Ti was very worried about him, but was not

allowed near him. She was distraught.

Mum had calmed her down and encouraged her to do sensible things like checking she had enough

food for her spell in isolation, getting reading material on her Kindle, telephoning Andrei regularly, all the sorts of things that Mums tell you to do. Ti was grateful and promised to be in touch soon.

The next call was that missed one to me.

"So, you feel guilty about waiting to return a call?" Nick sounded incredulous. "It happens all the

time. Even if you had rung back, it would not have altered what happened. You could not have

stopped her dying, my darling."

"I know, but she'd have heard a friendly voice. Dying alone, except for medical staff, must be so very

lonely. I'd have liked her to know that I was there for her."

Nick nodded. He took my hand and squeezed it.

"I'm sure she knows now."

My turn to nod.

"God, I hope so. Who was that at our wedding?"

"Probably just some onlooker, who looked a bit like Ti and who fled when you fainted. She must

have felt ashamed."

"Yes, I suppose so."

Lunch came then, a freebie in business class- and with wine too. After that we caught up on sleep

until the announcement came about our imminent landing in Larnaca. Looking out of the window I

could see land: coast, bays, mountains, lakes. All very inviting and exciting.

CHAPTER 7

It was already late afternoon, but the sun was shining and as we emerged from the plane we could

feel its warmth, very welcome after the chilly UK autumn.

"Oh, that is so nice to feel the sun on my face again. "

We walked from the plane to the terminal building, hand in hand, wheelie bag on each side. Life felt

good. We had thought that having travelled up front, we would be at the head of the queue for

passport examination. That meant that Nick could then slip to the car hire desk ahead of the rest

while I collected our checked-in bags. The car hire turned out to be more complicated. Nick had used

an online website to find the best deal, so the firm was not at a desk in the terminal; instead, we had

to wait in the car park at the Bay 6 sign for someone to come to us. This took nearly half an hour.

Nick was getting cross - but the bloke apologised profusely - there had been an accident in one of their cars, which had held him up. We were told to get into the battered old people carrier in which

he had arrived and were whisked to a nearby off-airport site. Here documents were checked, more

money paid, no we did not want additional insurance, thank you. Finally, we had our car, the keys

were handed over, a hand waved in the car's general direction, and we set off to find the right one.

The general lackadaisical approach was not inspiring so Nick photographed the car from every angle

to check for defects before we got in. All looked fine, it had done less than 1,000 miles and was

clean. No instruction book, no maps, just one piece of paper with vital information in the event of

any emergency. In fact, the little Suzuki was perfect - small enough to be economical with fuel, but

with enough room for us and our luggage. It also had air conditioning, which we learnt to love in the

heat of the day.

"Larnaca tonight, it is not far. I want to show you the museum there, the old town, the flamingo lake

and the tomb of Mohammed's aunt."

"Sounds great, thank you."

Just being beside him, aware of his masculine smell, his long body folded rather awkwardly into the

car seat, was my idea of heaven. For all I cared the journey could last for hours.

Getting to Larnaca took no time at all, finding our way to the hotel, even with the sat nav on my phone, was more complicated, largely because many streets were not named, at least not that we could see when driving past. Once off the highway there were lots of twisty little back streets in which we became lost. Seeing the same kafeneon with its old male clientele again and again,

reminded me of Bitter Lemons and the Tree of Idleness under which men whiled away the hours.

Nick had not read that book- so I explained and asked if there was any chance of our going to

Northern Cyprus.

"No, my darling. I am sorry but that is not possible. The car hire firm forbids it."

Eventually we found our hotel, but there were no parking spaces left. Nick sat in the car while I went

in and was directed to the nearest car park. We found it, then realized we had to bring our cases

back to the hotel with us, having not had the sense to leave them at Reception.

"Sorry Chloe, I should have thought this through."

I liked the fact that Nick apologized. He obviously thought he was in charge though, that appealed to

me somewhat less. "We should have thought this through," would have pleased me more.

"Don't leave anything valuable in the car, nothing should be in view." I was asserting my authority in

turn. Then the thought struck me: was I going to reproduce the only marriage that I knew well, the

competitive one of my parents? I resolved not to do that.

We rattled our cases over the uneven pavements, up and down multiple kerbs, until we were back at our LED- lit boutique hotel. I could hear the sea in the distance, a soothing regularity which eased my incipient crossness. By the time we reached our very clean, well- lit room I was recovered from my grouchy episode and happy to kick off my shoes and flop onto the bed. Nick locked the door, put the chain on as well and came and joined me.

Later we ventured out on foot to find supper and get an idea of our surroundings.

"We are close to the Church of St. Lazarus and to the beach," Nick informed me. "Saint Lazarus is supposed to be buried there."

"On the beach?"

He pretended to kick me. "Oh ye of little faith. You – who read Theology - should know better."

"Only joking. You began to sound like a guide- book."

"My apologies madame. I want to tell you about things that I know and love here."

"Thank you." I squeezed his arm affectionately.

We walked along the beachfront and chose a typical Cypriot restaurant in which to eat from the many available, all being heavily touted. The fish was fresh and delicious, the wine slipped down easily, the night breeze blew in from the sea, perfection. I refused sweet and coffee, feeling full already. Nick had both. Then Cyprus brandy on the house - we toasted our future together. We were happy, I was deliriously so.

The next day I looked on my phone to see what sites were available. The Archaeological Museum had just reopened after long closure - it looked ideal for me with its ancient artefacts; Nick seemed unwilling. He suggested that we split up for the morning: he would go diving and I could see the museum, then we'd meet for lunch. I felt miffed that so early on my honeymoon we would be apart, but had no wish to dive, so I agreed.

Once inside the museum turned out to be small: two rooms, but with treasures in glass cases. My favourite was a mediaeval vase with a man holding on to two horses- all looking as though drawn by Quentin Blake. At the inevitable shop I bought an etching of a massive urn on a hilltop – the assistant told me it was ancient Amathus, near

Limassol. The urn had been removed to the Louvre and replaced by a copy.

"Like the Elgin marbles, I guess."

She nodded.

"I want to go to London one day and see all those things in the British Museum that are not British at all."

Then it was my turn to nod, feeling ashamed.

On my way back to meet Nick I stepped into St Lazarus church. This was named for the Lazarus whom Jesus raised from the dead. I remembered that he was the brother of Martha and Mary of Bethany. After Jesus' death and resurrection, for some reason Lazarus had to flee Judea and he came to Cyprus where he became Bishop of Kition (now called Larnaca) thanks to Paul and Barnabas. He is said to have lived there for thirty more years and on his death was buried there for the second and last time. The Church of Agios Lazaros was built over his reputed (second) tomb.

It was a Byzantine structure with a surprisingly tall tower for a 9th century building, one that appeared to widen at the top. Inside it was cool and dark with the potent aroma of incense, beeswax and ancient stonework. A massive iconostasis was forced to stoop at the top by the curvature of the walls. I identified some of the saints pictured on it by their accoutrements: St. George – or was it St Michael? with a dragon, St Peter with the keys to the kingdom, St Jerome with his lion. The tomb of St Lazarus (why was he a saint?) was in the crypt, so I descended the stone stairs to see it. The mystical atmosphere, the thought of resurrection gave me hope and I lit a candle for Ti, placing it in the shallow dish of sand in the centre of other half burnt tapers.

"Don't be gone forever, please Ti."

Then I hurried to our rendezvous at the Tipsy Turtle as fast as my little legs could carry me.

CHAPTER 8

We left Larnaca that afternoon and drove to Limassol, making a detour to see the Salt Lake and the

Hala Sultan Tekke mosque. The lake had dried up, but Nick assured me that it would fill when the winter rains came and then the flamingos would return. Looking over the lake I could see the mosque, with a hill behind it, on top of which was what looked like a monastery.

The mosque was of great interest- from the guidebook which Nick had bought I learned that it had

been built in the 7th century on top of a Neolithic site at the spot where Mohammed's aunt, Umm Haram, had died after falling off a mule. It is a very important Muslim pilgrimage site, after Mecca, Medina and Al Aqsa mosque in Jerusalem. Unlike the St Lazarus church, the inside was almost bare, the main decoration being the tomb covered with a deep green cloth. The contrast was not unexpected: I had learnt in my Uni. Course that a mosque simply needs a space for prostration, and a mihrab which faces Mecca and shows the direction for prayer. Most also have a minaret, a dome and a place to wash before praying. The simplicity was refreshing. I already liked Cyprus for its sun, warmth and blue skies, now I was beginning to find it fascinating too.

We stayed on the coast road for a while, enjoying the views. Nick told me of his diving experience that morning. He had a PADI certificate so was able to join a dive without further training. He admitted that he'd booked the Zenobia wreck dive at the same time as our flights as it was something he'd wanted to do for ages. It occurred to me that this was perhaps why our honeymoon was in Cyprus. I forebore to ask whether he'd booked two places on the dive.

"It is among the top ten wreck dives in the world, my darling. An amazing experience. The Zenobia was a ferry. She capsized and sank about 40 years ago on her maiden voyage."

"Was anyone killed?"

He didn't know.

"Visibility is good- you can see lorries which fell off the deck, hundreds of them. The ship is on her side and fish and turtles swim in and out of it. Just amazing."

I made appreciative noises, feeling glad that I hadn't had to do it. Swimming is OK provided I keep my ears dry. My short limbs allow me to move swiftly through the water, a bit like a seal. Underwater stuff scares me though, gives me earache and I avoid it like the plague.

"I didn't think Zenobia had anything to do with Cyprus."

"Was she a real person?" asked Nick.

"Oh yes. She was known as the Queen of Palmyra."

"Where's that?"

"Behind us."

He looked in the car mirror.

"No, a long way behind us, in Northern Syria. Palmyra is an oasis on the Silk Route."

"What a lot you do know."

His smile took the sting out of the words. I found myself longing to plant a kiss on his mouth.

We joined the A1 motor way for the last section of the trip. I was amused that the exit signs, when I translated the Greek letters, said EXODUS. At no 21 we did just that and made our way to what Nick promised would be the luxury night of our trip- at the St Raphael Hotel. He'd chosen it because of the extensive COVID-19 precautions promised and for its beautiful setting near the marina.

The lobby lived up to our expectations, so did our room which had my essential: tea making facilities.

I made us a much-needed cup each while we settled in. Then we tested the bed, with much greater

success than the previous night, showered, changed and prepared to walk out to find supper. The

marina was lit by low sunlight, shadows were elongated, giving me my desired long legs. We strolled

hand in hand past the yachts which ranged from 30 footers to gin palaces, each choosing our

favourite for when we hit the jackpot.

A family, two adults and two children, were walking towards us. The little boy stared at me, then, in

a voice loud enough for me to hear, asked

"Is that lady a dwarf?"

I blushed and hurried Nick on, not wanting to hear the parental reply. At times I had taken it upon

myself to answer queries like that with the honest,

"Yes, I am a dwarf. I have a condition called achondroplasia which gives me short limbs."

Tonight though I just wanted to go on feeling the way that Nick had made me feel: normal and loved. Like Ti, he had not been bothered by my short limbs and large head so I could forget about them too. He squeezed my hand, then lifted it to his lips and kissed it, saying nothing.

I have always thought that my parents would have come to terms with having an unwanted child

much more easily if I had been normal looking. There are very few photos of me in babyhood or

infancy, most of those which exist were taken by Ti. Most early outings were with her, those with my parents were to the hospital. My achondroplasia is not inherited from my parents, apparently it resulted from a spontaneous mutation in the womb- so nobody's fault. Once at school it was largely forgotten, children are very accepting, so I thought little of it until my teens. Then fashion reared its ugly head and I suffered, along with all the other girls who weren't tall and stick thin. I compensated by dressing outlandishly.

"Hello love, where have you been?" My Mum asked one time- I was fifteen.

"Oxford Street. I bought a dress in the Top Shop sale."

"Oh, let's see."

I took the garish item out of its plastic bag and held it up against me.

"Is that the fashion now?"

"Yeah, do you like it?"

"Do you want me to be polite or honest?"

"Don't bother." I retreated to my room.

I don't think that I ever wore that dress.

Gran, bless her, tried hard to help. I only saw her in the holidays, but then sometimes I'd go and stay

with them for a week or two. She is lovely, small and elegant, well suited to her role as a diplomatic

wife, she is also very warm and caring. Somehow those genes didn't reach my Mum. Clothes fit my

torso, which is of normal proportions, but because of my short limbs, the length is excessive and

sleeves fall over my hands. At first Gran altered things to fit me, then taught me how to do it myself.

She taught me that plain colours or small patterns are best, big ones look silly on me.

One day she came to my bedroom one evening with a gift.

"Here you are darling, I found these in my jewellery box and thought they'd look better on you as

they match your eyes."

They were blue enamel and she was right about the match.

When she'd observed my face carefully, earrings in place, Gran said,

"Let's go shopping tomorrow for some material to match them. We can make you a dress."

Needlework at school had been my bête noire- but I was prepared to give it a go. We bought two

lots of material and one dress pattern. Gran showed me how to alter the pattern to fit me, then to

lay it onto the first lot of material, how to cut out the pieces and then helped me sew them together

using her old sewing machine. The result was not pristine, but I loved it.

"Now," said Gran," you are on your own with the second one. I'll be around if you need help."

I was so nervous I kept sweating all over the delicate paper pattern pieces. The pins seemed to want

to stick into me, not into the material and I got a small blood spot on it. However, I managed to lay

the pattern sections out on the fabric, cut round them,
then got stuck with what order to do things

next. Gran came and, instead of taking over and doing it, as
Mum would have done, she asked me

questions- so that I was able to work things out for myself.
She is just lovely, my Gran.

 Gran made my wedding dress from beautiful ivory silk, lent
me her best pearl earrings, and ordered

matching shoes with high heels to make me taller. It
brought us close together again, after a hiatus

while I was at Uni and had other fish to fry in the vacations.
She was delighted that I had found Nick-

or rather that he had found me.

"I love you so much," he said to me when the observant
child was out of earshot. I looked up at him,

smiling, he bent his head and we kissed, long and longingly,
right there on the street. I could feel myself tingling.

"My, my- that was a great PDA," he said afterwards.

"PDA?"

"Public Display of Affection, generally to be frowned upon, but sometimes very necessary."

"Too right."

We strolled on to find our supper.

CHAPTER 9.

Over our grilled calamari that evening we had taken it in
turns to look up Limassol in the guidebook,

having decided we could choose one thing each to see
before leaving. My choice was ancient

Amathus, a Neolithic site, then a major Cyprus fortress/city,
now mainly ruins on a hillside above a

nearby beach: Nick's was the motor museum with an
eclectic collection of cars.

 The next morning we swam in the still warm sea, me
keeping my ears dry with plugs, Nick swimming

underwater with snorkel and mask and exclaiming about
what he saw. After a mammoth breakfast

we set off for Amathus before it became too hot to climb
the hill. The ascent was fairly easy, my short stature seems
to help when climbing hills. On the top there was little left
to see, apart from large stones and a replica giant urn over
6 feet tall. Wikipedia informed us that

"Amathus was already almost deserted in 1191 when Richard Plantagenet won Cyprus. Stones were

removed and used for building in Limassol. Stone blocks from Amathus were also used in 1869 for

the construction of the Suez Canal."

And, more worryingly that we might have slept over graves:

" it is thought that some of the hotels are on top of the Amathus necropolis."

Down the hill there were more extensive Roman remains and the wooden port structures were

visible below the water. We arrived back at sea level hot and sweaty.

"Let's get a drink," said Nick.

"Good idea."

We found a small tavern and sat under the awning in the shade. I asked for water, Nick wanted that plus a Greek coffee and something sweet to eat. The waiter advised the locally made baklava, which

arrived looking even stickier than we felt.

"Oh, it's delicious. Try some sweetheart."

He passed me a small spoonful. I took the spoon and put it gently to my lips, then removed it

hurriedly.

"Sorry, not for me."

"Don't you like it? Is it too sweet?"

"No, it's got pistachios in it. I can't eat them, I'm allergic to them."

"How did you know so quickly?"

"They make my lips tingle almost immediately. It's a useful test if you're not sure whether something

has pistachios in it or not."

"What would have happened if you'd eaten that spoonful?"

"I'm not sure. It's been a long time since I had a reaction- but they used to be severe. I have an Epi

pen with me always, just in case."

"Heavens, is that the rescue pen thing?"

"Yes. It has adrenalin in it and can save lives."

I opened my handbag, brought out the adrenalin pen and showed it to him. He took some time to

read the instructions, then said,

"So, I would have to hold it up like this, take off the blue top then thrust it into your thigh, even

through your clothes?"

"Yes, then hold it there for a slow count of 10, then remove it and rub the place where you injected

it. I should be lying on the ground with my legs propped up."

"O.K. Is there a You tube video?"

"Lots- here you go."

I handed him my phone to watch.

"OK, I now know what to do if you have a reaction."

He thought, then said "You should have told me before- what if something had happened on the plane?"

"Oh, I am very careful. It's only pistachios and cashew that I can't eat- and they are not common."

"Why those two?"

"I don't know. I think they grow on similar kinds of tree."

My childhood had been punctuated with trips to hospital – initially terrifying ones as an emergency

for anaphylaxis and/or asthma, then to routine clinics for allergy diagnosis and testing, progress

monitoring and checking that I still had my EpiPen and knew how to use it. Fortunately, as I grew

everything improved and I had not been seen in a clinic for a couple of years. The paediatric

department had bid me farewell when I reached sixteen and had passed me on to the adult allergy service. They seemed more detached, so I stopped going, but I still used my asthma inhaler and nasal spray religiously every single day without fail, as I'd realised they were what kept me well. I'd allowed myself to push allergy to the back of my mind, so it had not occurred to me to warn Nick.

"Let's go and see those old cars," I said, wanting to change the subject rather than from any auto-

enthusiasm. Nick was eager though, so we paid the bill, avoided the free Cyprus brandy, and set off in our hire car. For me the visit was brief, I liked the look of old models, especially when they were shiny deep red or yellow, but had no interest in their mechanics or performance. Nick was in auto heaven, discussing cylinder numbers, horsepower and other recondite details with two other male visitors.

I found a cool place to sit and opened the guidebook. My theology course had barely mentioned

Cyprus- but it seemed that lots of relevant events had taken place on the island. St Paul had visited, with Barnabas- and they had been stoned in Paphos. The pillar was said to be still there in the

grounds of a very old church. Also interesting was the cult of Aphrodite on Cyprus: I wanted to see

the place where she was worshipped in old Paphos- and the rocks where she was said to have been

born from the sea. I was delighted that Nick had chosen the island of love for our honeymoon.

Thinking of that made me remember Ti and that led to thoughts of my mother- with whom I'd

promised to keep in touch. I think she feared losing me on Cyprus too and she was wary of Nick. The

latter I knew to be true from the way she spoke to him and of him. She had obviously not expected

anyone to fall in love with me, hardly surprising since she'd found it hard to love me herself.

I took out my phone and rang her.

"Hello darling," she said.

"Hi Mum, just letting you know we're fine. Cyprus is really fascinating- there's lots that I want to

see."

"I wish we'd all gone there to see Ti, while she was alive." Her voice was regretful, but she

brightened.

"How was your flight?"

I explained about Club Class and the views of the island as we flew along it to Larnaca, then told her

about the things I'd seen.

"My darling I am so glad that you are happy."

"Oh I am, Mum, I really am."

"One thing- are you going to Paphos?"

"Yes, certainly we are. Nick has arranged for us to stay in an Airbnb at Sea Caves, but we'll go

through Paphos to get there."

"Could you do something for me, darling?"

"Sure, if I can. What is it?"

"Ti had a lawyer there. He is supposed to be doing the probate for me as I was down as her

executor– but it is taking an awfully long time. We correspond by e–mail– but I don't think that we

always understand each other and his secretary lacks perfect English. I don't know why it should be

complicated, Ti had very little as far as I know. If you could pay him a visit and speak to him in person

I think that would help. I'll cover any costs."

"Yes, I could do that. Can you let me have his details?"

"I'll e-mail them to you, darling. Thank you so much. Goodbye now."

"Goodbye Mum."

Nick emerged from the last room of cars.

"Hey, did you get fed up?"

"No, I had the guidebook to read and I just spoke to Mum."

"How is she?"

"Fine. She wants me to visit a lawyer about Ti when we get to Paphos. I said I would."

"Oh, OK."

"You don't have to come. It will probably be boring."

"OK. Are you ready to rumble?"

"Yes, let's go. Where to?"

"Well, now for something completely different. Just wait and see."

We returned to the Suzuki and Nick drove us to the motorway, but then soon turned off to the right

and headed upwards towards the distant mountains. The road, straight at first, with traffic lights,

streetlamps, the accoutrements of a city, soon changed its nature and became a narrow switchback,

constantly rising. Long shadows cast by the setting sun interrupted the amber glow inside the car from time to time each time we passed a tree. It felt like a race against time- could we go fast

 enough towards the sunlit uplands to keep the sun in our sky? The movement and the sunlight were

hypnotic and Nick's presence beside me so wonderful that I felt that I never wanted this journey to

end. But end it did- in a cool, upland place with plentiful aromatic trees and almost alpine buildings.

"We have arrived."

"Where are we?"

"Troodos, up in the mountains. We are close to Mount Olympus."

"Home of the Gods?"

"Probably."

"Looks lovely." The sun was no longer visible, but its light still bathed the world in a rosy glow.

Warm it was not, though. I opened the car door and chill air swept in, at once both surprising and welcome.

"Oh, it's so fresh. And it smells wonderful."

"It feels like my homeland. Although my parents moved to the UK and brought us, me up there, I still feel very connected to Cyprus. We came to my grandparents for holidays most years."

"Where did your grandparents live?"

"In a village near Paphos. I will show you when we are there. Tomorrow we can walk here."

"Oh, I only have trainers, will they do?"

"Yes, it is not difficult territory."

The Troodos Hotel was welcoming, if a little spartan. I was glad of the chance of a shower and a

change of clothes. Nick said he'd go out for a stroll while I used the bathroom. Once out of the

shower, I was able to hear voices from the rear of the building. One of them was Nick's voice,

speaking what sounded like Greek. A word that I caught was "dikigóros". The reply was brief and higher pitched, it could have been a female voice. The small high window was frosted so I could see

nothing.

I was dressed and sitting applying my make up in front of the mirror when Nick returned.

"My darling you look lovely," he said appreciatively, putting his hands on my shoulders and bending

to kiss the top of my head.

"And you smell lovely too."

My heart melted again.

"Thank you."

I turned and stood up to face him- or rather to face his chest. He stooped to find my lips with his.

The kiss was gentle at first, then became more intense and soon we were on the bed together,

undoing all the good work I had done in getting ready.

The conversation I'd overheard was forgotten.

CHAPTER 10

It has not entirely left my mind however and the next morning I found myself scanning the

breakfast tables for a lone female. There was no- one obvious. I wondered whether to ask Nick- but

decided not to do so. I did not want him to think that I had been snooping on him.

We visited the little museum and found that we were at one of the most interesting places on

earth, geologically speaking. The ground is made of the sea floor which had been forced upwards

about 20 million years ago. Erosion of this means that the Earth's mantle, normally several

kilometres below the surface, is now exposed and can be walked on. The area has advanced the

understanding of current processes taking place under the oceans and of the collision of the Earth's

tectonic plates. I found it fascinating, but not fully comprehensible- Nick seemed to understand it better- and pointed out different types of rock when we did our walk down the Caledonian Trail

afterwards. Fortunately I am pretty fit- I do yoga every day and run twice a week- because the walk

was by a stream, which had to be crossed repeatedly, going downhill on the way out, but uphill for a

few miles coming back.

Fortunately Nick stopped at intervals to look through his binoculars at birds.

"Hey love, look – it's a Griffon vulture!"

The name brought memories of Alice in Wonderland- but the reality was a huge handsome bird seen

from below in flight: wings with white bands amongst the dark and finger- like feather projections at

each end, legs covered in feathered versions of Victorian ladies' pantaloons.

"Wow!"

I got out my phone and took a burst of pictures. Nick had his Nikon with a telephoto lens and busied himself adjusting it for so long that he missed the photo.

"Shit!"

"Did you get it Chloe?"

I showed him my phone- one or two of the shots were pretty good. Nick was impressed.

"It's amazing what these things can do," he said. "I should use mine more often."

Once back in Troodos we got back into the little Suzuki and drove the long and winding road

downwards towards the coast. This was different one to the one from Limassol, veering more to the

west, but was also beautiful. I realized that potamos meant river- so a hippo is a river horse, hippo

potamos. The river Xeros told one everything necessary to know about it. I loved learning odd bits of

Greek and said so to Nick.

"You have a wonderful enquiring mind, my darling" he responded, delighting me.

Then, upsettingly,

"I hope it never gets you into trouble."

I turned my face down to look at the map, hiding how cross I felt. The road we were taking wound its

way down towards the coast, alongside the river Diarizos (which I didn't try to translate). Just before

it ended there was something called the Sanctuary of Aphrodite near a place called Kouklia. There

was a diamond marking the spot, indicating an archaeological site and monument. I asked Nick

about it.

"Oh, it is extremely ancient. Apparently folk used to come from all round the Mediterranean to

worship there, thousands of years ago."

"Could we stop and look at it?"

He hesitated, turning his wrist to see his watch.

"Probably, if we speed up a bit."

The twists and bends in the road were now taken faster and I began to regret asking for the visit.

We slowed down for a village, Pano Archimandrita.

"Interesting name", I said, partly to divert Nick's attention so he did not put his foot down so hard again.

"Why?"

"Well, an archimandrite is an abbot in the orthodox church, a superior celibate priest in charge of

other priests. "In charge of the sheepfold" is what the name means, literally."

"Little Miss Clever, you are spot on. There is a legend that says hundreds of them were walled up

here in a cave and left to die. Apparently they had fled from Syria and were refugees."

For a few moments I was too horrified to speak, then I said,

"How horrible. Is it true? What's the evidence?"

"I don't know. There are hundreds of legends in Cyprus, probably mostly false, but we don't treat refugees much better now, do we?"

"What do you mean?"

"I was thinking of those poor people who dies of
asphyxiation in the back of a lorry on their way to

the UK."

He was right. The world had still not learnt to share.

The bends grew fewer as the land flattened out towards
the coast and soon Kouklia announced itself

on a sign. There were stone houses, still decorated with
geraniums and bougainvillea, one or two

cafes and a small shop- and soon what looked like a small
fortress in the distance. It was 4.20pm- the

guard in the gatehouse grunted that we had only 40
minutes, but sold us two beautiful tickets, each

with a photo of an Aphrodite statue, for what seemed like
a bargain price compared to UK sites.

Nick thoughtfully added a small guidebook to the purchase,
then handed it to me.

"Thank you, sweetheart." The Clever Clogs was evened out.

At first I was disappointed- there was a large area with traces of a few walls still obvious, but it was

hard to work out what it would have looked like. However once inside the fortress- which was 14th

century Venetian- the film explained much about the site. In the little time left I marvelled at the

reality: an iconic black phallic symbol which had been worshipped there for generations and at the

wonderful stone baths. There was a beautiful, vaulted stone hall beneath the museum, empty and

perfect for a wedding, I thought- shame that we'd already had ours. On our way back to the car I

found several large boards explaining the cult of Aphrodite on Cyprus, something my theology

course had failed to include, perhaps because the temple maidens were effectively prostitutes.

"Thank, Nick, that was fascinating," I said as we returned to the car." Would you like me to drive for a bit?"

"No, my darling, thank you. It gets a bit complicated from here so best if I carry on for now."

"Fine, as long as you are not tired."

"Driving does not tire me, I enjoy it."

How different from me, I thought. Driving to me was a necessity, never an enjoyment. I was always

aware that I was in charge of a machine which could kill.

The final leg of the journey was indeed complicated. We briefly returned to the motorway until its

end in a large roundabout at the edge of Paphos, which stretched downwards towards the sea as

well as straight ahead. That was the route we took, zipping along a dual carriageway in the fast lane,

through several traffic lights – it dawned on me that I'd seen very few before in Cyprus, such a

change from London- then turning right , then left onto a smaller road. Then we travelled as Dad says" in the general direction of along", more or less parallel to the coast, but on the hillsides above

it. There were several villages, each seemed to have an ancient church and there were interesting

- looking brown signs to ancient sites. Nick glanced at me.

"Don't worry, my darling. We can visit all of them at leisure while we are staying at Sea Caves."

I loved the way he could read my mind.

Finally, after more twists and turns, we arrived at our destination- an Airbnb rental flat in a small

block, a couple of hundred yards from the sea. It was a peaceful looking place, a two-storey block,

not very exciting to look at from the outside. Nick found the key safe, put in the code which he'd

been sent and fished out a set of keys on a ring. The one marked H opened the front door and we

entered an echoing, marble staired hallway. The stairs in front of me went both up and down as the

flat was built on a hillside.

"Which way?" I asked.

"It's number 202," he paused peering upwards, "up there, in the middle."

We climbed the stairs, inserted key F and, after several twists, the door opened into a small lobby. A

bookcase faced us, with lots of interesting looking books, CDs and some pottery in a bright

Mediterranean blue. I started to check the book titles, Nick had gone on through the little kitchen

and called,

"Hey, come and look at this."

An archway led from the kitchen into a small sitting room, I went through it and Nick moved to one

side so I could see the view through the double glass doors. It was stunning- an expanse of sea and

sky, some of it the same blue I had just been admiring in the pottery.

"Wow, that's fantastic!"

We opened the doors and went out onto the long balcony which extended across the front of the

flat. From here the horizon extended from Paphos on the left to somewhere indeterminate on the

right- so far that it appeared to be slightly curved. There were what looked like two wrecked ships,

one quite close, listing onto the shore; the other improbably moored in a large bay near Paphos.

There was another block of our complex immediately to the right below us, with an ugly flat roof

with satellite dishes and solar- heated water containers, but one's eye was drawn away to the

glorious seascape.

Nick turned to me.

"Is this what you wanted?"

"Oh, yes my darling. It's perfect, thank you, thank you."

We kissed, oblivious to the possibility of watchers. The glass doors to the bedroom were locked from the inside so we had to go back through the kitchen to reach it, shutting the flat door on the way.

The beautifully- arranged bed was soon satisfactorily rumpled and then we lay there quietly, tired,

turning our heads to gaze at the sea, listening to its susurration against the rocks.

"I like not being in a hotel."

"Me too."

Nick bestirred himself.

"I'll bring in our cases."

I lay there, perfectly content. I don't think that I had ever been so happy.

"Here's your tea."

I must have been dozing. Nick's voice sounded gently amused as he deposited a mug on my side of

the bed- the window side.

"Oh, thank you love."

I stretched, yawned, and struggled up into a seated position, propped by a pillow against the

headboard. I sipped the tea, which was hot, strong and delicious, just as I liked it.

"OK?" Nick asked.

"Very OK, thank you. Just right."

"Good. We aim to please."

He sat beside me, putting his mug on the other bedside cabinet, then put his arm round me.

"Mrs. Nicolaou, you and I are going to be a success together."

"I'll drink to that." The tea tasted even better.

CHAPTER 11

And we were- a success, that is. The days passed very pleasantly. It was still sunny and warm enough

to swim in the sea and in the pool below the flat. We did the former in the day and the latter each

evening, with sightseeing and meals out sandwiched in between. I learnt the word "Chalcolithic "

and visited those very ancient sites as well as more modern Roman and Greek ones. The mosaics in

Neo Paphos were fantastic, easily the best I'd ever seen. One had what looked like a traffic light

depicted on it, probably a serving dish in reality, but I took a photo and What's Apped it home.

I kept wondering if Ti had seen these things and enjoyed them but said nothing of this to Nick.

One day in late afternoon I was semi- lying post-swim on a lounger, in a sun- warmed alcove of the pool, watching the pigeons on the telegraph wires changing the pattern from Doh Ray Me to

Rachmaninov as more and more arrived. Nick had walked back down to the sea to snorkel. Sunlight

bouncing from the surface of the water was so bright that I shut my eyes. Then it was playing over

my closed eyelids, making patterns. I was half- way to being asleep, totally content. Life was good.

Suddenly I heard Ti 's voice saying my name. My eyes snapped open: no- one was there. My heart

was thumping, I felt weird. Was this her attempt at contact from beyond the grave? I stayed there

waiting, hoping, until the sun went behind a tree, it became colder and I climbed the stairs to our

flat.

The next morning Nick announced that it was a good day for the Avagas Gorge, being slightly cloudy

and less hot.

"OK, what is that place?"

"It's a river gorge running down to the sea from the hills above. It is in the Akamas wilderness to the

north of here and there is a great walk up it. The water has gouged a deep channel in the rocks- at

times it is almost a tunnel. You will love it."

He showed me on the map.

"How long is the walk?"

"Oh, I don't actually know that- but it used to take me a couple of hours to walk from the bottom up

to the village at the top. It's a scramble in parts, so quite slow going."

"I haven't brought any walking boots."

"You will be fine in trainers. If it gets too difficult, we can turn back. Bring a sunhat and some water."

"OK."

My enthusiasm for this venture was somewhat muted. My short legs are not well suited to scrambling over rough ground, but I wanted to be with Nick in a place that he liked, so I donned my

only pair of jeans, trainers, a T-shirt and my sunhat, slathered myself with sun lotion and filled the

small rucksack with the map, a bottle of water, some bread, cheese and two apples my phone, a

towel and a 20 euro note.

"Ready when you are," I announced.

"Very intrepid looking," Nick smiled, pulled me to him, turned up the hat brim and kissed my

forehead gently.

"Let's go."

In the car he said,

"With your penchant for understanding Greek you might like to know the origin of the name

Avagas."

"Oh yes, do tell."

"Avga means eggs, so it's likely that early man collected eggs from the cliffs- or possibly I suppose

from the nearby turtle beach."

"A turtle beach?"

"Sure, Lara Beach, we can see that too, afterwards. Have a swim perhaps"

 That sounded more my type of place.

The road suddenly turned in to a rutted track which wound sharply down and round to cross a small

river valley, only to climb up again and continue north. I was glad that the little car was not our own

as I could hear stones clanging against the bodywork and feel the juddering from the uneven

surface. The sea was close on our left now and suddenly we turned right and accelerated uphill on

an even more rutted bumpy track, passing what looked like a castle situated on the hilltop.

"It's a restaurant", Nick said," called Viklari, The Last Castle. Open at the weekend- we could come for Sunday lunch if you like."

"Sounds good- the views must be lovely."

The track again headed downhill and finally, to my relief we stopped in a small car park. I stepped

down from the car and gazed at the scenery which had changed from rather desolate seashore to a

more verdant narrow valley between almost vertical rocks, with flat- topped cliffs on either side. The

whole scene could have been out of a movie set in the time of dinosaurs, I half expected to see an

anachronistic fur bikini -clad Raquel Welch emerge from the trail leading away from us into the

gorge.

"Wow, this is unexpected."

"Thought you'd like it."

I took a sip of water, put the bottle down, then hoisted the little rucksack onto my back.

"I'll carry that love."

Nick took it, lengthened the straps, and shouldered it. His binoculars were hanging round his neck,

 making him look very professional.

"Let's go."

We set off at a brisk pace, walking up the valley, along a path dotted with trees and small plants,

many of which bore labels. Stopping to read them meant that I was soon lagging behind. Nick

stopped to look at some birds. He turned round to show me and realised I was some way behind.

"Sorry, I was learning about the plants." I said when I caught up." "Oh, grey wagtails!"

"Well spotted. You know that no- one knows why they wag their tails?"

I shook my head and thought how much I liked having this interesting, even slightly nerdy, man as my husband.

We walked on and the track became narrower and more winding. We had to cross the stream – it certainly did not justify the name of river. Then cross back...and again and again.... Now we were

climbing steadily and having to use stepping stones to get over the water. Nick, with his long legs

was far more agile and far speedier than me. It was a relief to arrive at a part where the two sides of

the gorge practically met overhead, shutting out the light. The swirls on the side walls showed how

the passageway had been carved out by the water passing through.

"Nick, please could I get my phone?"

He handed me the rucksack.

I took a photo of him, standing on a rock in the narrow passage.

"This must have happened ages ago when there was a lot more water."

"Oh, if it rains hard then this place can flood in minutes."

"Really?"

I must have sounded doubtful because Nick went on to explain that people had been killed here by a

flash flood, the sudden rush of storm water down the hill, knocking them down and drowning them.

"You should never come here when rain threatens in the hills."

I looked up anxiously, but very little sky was visible. The walk no longer seemed such fun. Nick was

about to set off again. I remembered something.

I looked in the rucksack. As I had just remembered, the water was not there, I had accidentally left it

beside the car.

"Oh sugar, I've left the water behind- by the car."

"You could drink from the stream."

"And get dysentery as a bonus."

I sighed.

"Nick, I am very thirsty. You are so much better than me at this jumping, hopping and skipping from rock to rock that I am holding you back. Why don't I go back and have some water, maybe find Lara

beach then I'll return and meet you when you come down again."

"If I go alone then I'd like to try to get out the other end and walk up to Kano Panos."

"Well, if you do give me a ring and I can drive round to collect you. Keep the rucksack, there's some

food in it but give me the map and the car keys please. Give me a ring anyway when you decide

what you are going to do."

"You're sure?"

"Yes, certain sure."

"All right, my darling. I'll see you later."

He tossed me the car keys and thankfully I caught them. Then Nick was off, like a gazelle, leaping

from rock to rock. I felt a mixture of love and envy sweep over me as I turned to go back down to the car.

Like all return journeys it did not seem as far as it had on the way out and I felt a fool for having

given up so easily. I was just pulling the car keys out of my pocket to retrieve the water when I again

heard a familiar voice calling my name.

"Chloe! Chloe!"

I looked around, it came from a Land Rover parked nearby. A dark- haired woman was leaning out of

the driver's window and beckoning to me. There was something familiar about her movements. I

walked towards the vehicle.

"Hello," I said. "Do I know you?"

Close to, those green eyes were unmistakable. I stopped dead in my tracks.

It was Ti.

CHAPTER 12

I was incapable of speech or movement.

"Upsadaisy Whoa! Chloe, get in quickly for God's sake before somebody sees us."

The familiar wording broke the spell and I did as she asked, opening the rear door and getting into

the seat. The Land Rover was moving before I had a chance to find my seat belt.

"Sorry Chloe, we have to get away from here, then I will explain. Buckle up, but slide down in your

seat so no- one sees you."

I did as I was asked, just like always with Ti.

We bumped back over the hill by the Last Castle, down nearly to the beach, but then turned right to

go further north.

"Where are we going? What about Nick?"

"We're going somewhere safe, not for long. Nick will be fine."

I registered that she hadn't asked who the hell was Nick- so perhaps she knew.

Was she real? I didn't think a ghost could drive like this- and anyway my theology course had done

away with my belief in ghosts altogether, along with beliefs of most kinds.

"We're just passing Lara beach where the turtles lay their eggs," Ti announced.

"There are a few cars there, after that this road is usually pretty empty- I'll find a good spot, then

stop. Are you OK in the back there?"

"Battered black and blue, but otherwise fine."

"Good girl."

We continued for a few minutes longer, then turned right and bumped even more uphill. Eventually

turned the vehicle round and stopped. The silence and lack of movement was blissful.

I sat up and looked around. We were on a hillside, behind two trees, with a wide expanse of land below us and beyond that the sea. There were no cars, no obvious people.

 "Can we talk now?"

"Yes, my darling, we can. Climb into the front and I'll give you a big hug first."

We clung together for a while, so happy to be both alive and together. Then Ti kissed my forehead,

reminding me of Nick, and said,

"I owe you an explanation."

"You sure do. How come you are alive? What were you doing making me faint at my wedding?

Those are your starters for 10."

Ti laughed.

"No, I need to go back much further than that. I have to tell you the whole story."

CHAPTER 13

Ti's story.

"I suppose it begins some years ago, when my brilliant career as a singer and recording artist failed

to materialize. I was broke and miserable, so I went home to Mum and Dad."

Ti cast her mind back to that day.

" I knocked on the door before peeping round it. Entering the Holy of Holies is a bit like going into the

head's study at boarding school: one feels nervous, even though it was my Dad in there. He is still a

figure to be reckoned with, even in his sixties. Silver grey hair, an austerely handsome face, crisp

white shirt, beautiful suit, Eton tie- this was in the pre-COVID era when occasional working from

home still meant dressing the part. His head was bent, spectacles perched on his nasal bridge,

looking intently at the document in his hand. He looked up, saw me and smiled,

"Felicity, come in darling. How can I help?"

Someone once told me that this is the way to disarm people – to offer them something positive right

from the word go. Dad had obviously used it to his advantage throughout his diplomatic career.

"I wonder if I could talk to you about my future- or rather the lack of it!"

"Go on my darling, spill those beans."

Dad turned his gaze upon me, tipping his head slightly to one side- a listening pose.

I told him that my singing work had more or less dried up. The album I had slaved over had been well

reviewed, but had not sold many copies, so there would not be a second one. Younger, prettier girls

with good voices were coming out of the woodwork- so my future was certainly not bright, not orange, more grey.

Dad murmured sympathetically,

"You deserve better, my darling."

I ploughed on with my question.

"Do you think that I should go to Uni?"

"Do you want to?"

"Yes, I think that now I would make good use of it."

"Then you shall."

I smiled and breathed out with relief.

"And you'd fund me? Until I could pay you back?"

"No need for that, repayment I mean. Yes. We'd fund you."

I moved round his desk, clear as always, apart from the family photo and his computer, and hugged

him, kissing the top of his head.

Oh, Dad, I'm so grateful. Thank you so much."

He paused, looked closely at me, said slowly,

"Your course would start when?"

"Oh, in Autumn- September or October, I think."

"Then there is something you could do for me between now and the start of Uni."

"What?"

"A little bit of observation. Let me see if I can sort it out, then I'll tell you more. Off you go now, tell

Mum I'll be out for lunch today please."

"Sure, will do. Thanks Dad." He was already looking at the document again, I was dismissed.

 Mum, when I found her, was not displeased about Dad missing lunch.

"Oh, good," she said. "You and I can make do with luftovers (a family word) if you don't mind. That'll

clean out the fridge nicely and allow me to get on with this."

My mother is a marvel. Highly intelligent she'd abandoned St Paul's aged 16, telling them they'd

taught her all she needed to know, and went to Art School. She'd later taught there, mainly theatre

design. She is small, always elegant, with a quirky, humorous face that can look beautiful when she *allows it to relax. That happens rarely as she is constantly on the go, doing something or other that*

she finds of great interest. What that is varies according to time of day, season of the year, her

mood, whatever. This day she was painting in her attic room, a landscape looking nothing like the

view in front of her window.

"Where is that? "

"Wales, the Golden Valley, one of my favourite places there. It's from a photograph and my

memories."

I could see the photo now, pinned to the easel. It showed a winding river passing through fields lit by

the setting sun.

"It's glorious."

"Mmm." She applied more paint to the canvas.

Mum was obviously not wanting to talk, so I left her and returned downstairs to read the paper with a second cup of coffee. I felt like a spare part. What a disappointment I must be to them. At least

Katherine has done well in her career, that must be some comfort to the aged Ps.

That evening Dad returned and asked me to join him at 6ish for a drink before supper in his office. I

knocked and entered, again feeling like the naughty schoolgirl I used to be. Dad was very welcoming,

pouring a G&T for me from the selection of bottles on his side cabinet, sitting me down comfortably

on the sofa. I knew something bad was coming.

"My darling I had a chat to someone at work today and we both think that you might be just the

person we need."

"Sounds good. What are the job specifications?"

"Someone who can sing, doesn't get seasick, speaks Russian, can chat to people easily and is willing

to pass on information gained."

"Seasick? Where is the job?"

"On the Queen Mary. The singer they had booked has suddenly had to back out because of illness, so

they need a replacement soon."

I nodded. That sounded my sort of job.

"Who am I supposed to chat up?"

"This chap."

Dad slipped a photo out of his jacket inside pocket and gave it to me. The man pictured was

unsmiling in the way of passport photos, even so he was undeniably handsome in an Omar Sharif

fashion.

"Arabic?"

"Georgian. He was KGB at one time, got to know Putin there and they became friends. When the

Soviet Union fell apart he managed to hit the big time, buying up gas sources and pipelines, probably

with help from Putin. He was in the "Troika Laundromat"
and funnelled billions of USD through the

system. Corruption was rife. They stayed pals for some
years, but recently appear to have fallen out.

Putin makes a habit of allowing his mates to become
oligarchs, provided they keep him supplied with

a proportion of their proceeds. The proportion has risen
gradually – hence the numbers of Russians

bailing out, leaving for the UK, USA, now Cyprus with its
golden passport system. This chap calling

himself Andrei Komarov, not his real name, went secretly to
Australia, but they won't let him stay.

Andrei is leaving on the Queen Mary shortly as he hopes to
evade detection by not using an airport.

He's booked as far as Southampton, having made discreet
enquiries about asylum in the UK. We'd

like you to debrief him, as unobtrusively as possible, on the
boat and report to me everything you find

out each day. I'll get back to you with further questions,
areas of concern etc."

"Sounds interesting. I'm willing to have a go."

"Thank you, my darling. It is all a bit time- sensitive. You will
need to return to the UK tomorrow for

some preparatory training about the questions to ask and
how to contact me, then you can get on

the boat in Singapore. I really appreciate this, Felicity."

Dad bent and kissed the top of my head.

"Let's go and have supper with Mum."

Ti came round from her reverie and continued,

"Dad found me a sort of Mata Hari job."

"Sounds very unsavoury. Did Gramps know what he was
letting you in for?"

"My darling, what do you think Gramps has been doing all
his working life?"

Somewhere a penny dropped.

"He's a spy isn't he? Not a real diplomat at all."

Ti nodded.

"That had dawned on me after I read a book about Kim Philby. It was obvious that most embassies

are used as covers for spying. Gramps' speciality was Russia, now it's Eastern Europe." She paused.

"My target was one of the new breed of super criminal-many emerging from the Soviet Union after

its break up. My ability to speak Russian was a big plus."

"So you accepted?"

"Yes. There wasn't much else on offer- and I was intrigued by the job. They sent me for brief training,

I passed and off I went sailing away."

Ti paused again, then asked.

"How long have we got?"

"I'm not sure. Nick was going to ring me when he's decided whether he's going all the way through

the gorge or turning back."

"There's been a big rock fall and no- one can get through anymore- so once he reaches that he'll

ring. Please answer without mentioning me. Nick must know nothing of this. "

She thought for a moment.

"You have your car keys?"

"Yes."

"Message him now and tell him you have walked to the beach. Ask him to wait for you by the car."

I nodded. While I was doing that Ti continued.

"I met Andrei on the Queen Mary. He was a person of interest to MI6, and I was asked to find out as

much as possible about him. He was doing the full cruise from Australia to the UK, sailing under his

pseudonym. I joined the ship in Singapore for a week or so's work singing in the evenings. After every

show I've always found it hard to go straight to bed and sleep- so I'd got into the habit of going to one of the bars for a nightcap, a chat to the barman and a wind down before turning in. Andrei was

in the bar on my first night onboard. I had just sat down on a barstool when he came up to me and

thanked me, saying how much he'd enjoyed the show and offering to buy me a drink. That was par

for the course- but I recognized his face as the person in whom the Service was interested. He'd

made a fortune when the USSR fell apart, largely by buying up gas production plants. They wanted to

know whether he was still "in" with Putin and what his future plans were, whether he'd want asylum

in the UK."

"Of course I said,

"Thank you. I'd love a gin and tonic."

"He introduced himself as Andrei, not his real name, I asked him to call me Bella, my stage name, and

away we went, chatting nineteen to the dozen. His English was good, so I did not let on that I spoke

Russian at first. From the start I found him very attractive, he was an Omar Sharif type, expressive

eyes, warm, sympathetic. I could not believe that he was a criminal. "

The bartender put on some music and "I only have eyes for you" was sung. It seemed to express the

situation remarkably accurately.

Ti could have been describing my initial feelings about Nick. I said nothing, just listened while she

detailed their shipboard romance which had progressed at warp speed because she'd told Andrei

that she was leaving the ship after her booking was over. She passed to London some of the

information they had requested: no, he was no longer a friend of Putin; no, he was not intending to

return to Russia, yes, there was some unease in the Putin camp. As yet she did not know whether he'd ask for asylum once the ship docked in Southampton. He'd persuaded her to stay longer on

board with him after her singing contract finished. She moved into his stateroom. They spent every

hour together until, when the ship docked in Limassol, Andrei persuaded her to become his second

wife in a ship's ceremony just before they disembarked, using his real identity. After that he'd taken

her into the city, visited an estate agent and arranged to rent a house there by the sea, starting that

 night. They returned to the ship, collected their belongings, and became wedded landlubbers.

"At first it was blissful. We hit it off together so well. He was relaxed and happy, so was I."

 Ti looked dreamy.

"What happened to his first wife?" I asked, very suspicious of this rapid romance, despite my own

having been only slightly slower.

"She died of cancer some years ago, after they'd been married 5 years without having any children.

Andrei was devastated. It took him ages to dare to love again- I was the first person he'd loved after

her."

"What happened next?"

"One day Andrei suddenly changed. I don't know why- or didn't then. He became anxious,

withdrawn. I asked him what was wrong- but he just smiled and said it was a business matter that he

needed to sort out. He told me to keep a small bag packed with essentials as we might leave soon

and gave me a set of clothes for travelling. I contacted my handler in MI6, she knew very little—

except that a Russian mafia hitman had recently been spotted entering Cyprus at Larnaca airport.

That night we upped and left the rented villa in a taxi, taking a couple of suitcases with us. The taxi took us to the airport at Paphos, from where we apparently had tickets to fly to Moscow. We

checked in, put the suitcases on the belt to go into the hold, then walked away – but Andrei suddenly

steered me towards the loos, handing me a package.

"Put these on and meet me in the car park, zone C, no 4 in 5 minutes please."

The package contained spectacles, a wig and a thin reversible jacket. He'd had spy training too. I

obeyed his instructions. C4 bay held a dark car with Cyprus plates, Andrei was in the driving seat. I

got in and we sped off, along back roads, to Sea Caves. On the way he told me that he was now

considered an enemy of the Russian state because he was refusing demands to sell gas at prices

determined by it and to pay exorbitant state dues. He'd pretended to agree go to Moscow to speak

face to face with Putin but knew that this was an invitation to imprisonment or worse. Instead, we were going to lie low in Cyprus and hope for regime change in Russia. He'd arranged for a couple

looking like us to take another flight from Paphos to the UK on fake passports. The female had been

given the same set of clothes as me. That way he hoped to divert any pursuers. The house we were

going to in Sea Caves was now in the name of a company with no obvious connections to Andrei, but

somehow he'd managed to use its purchase to obtain a "golden EU passport." I was horrified that I'd

landed myself in the middle of a nightmare, but I loved him and did not want to leave him.

That's why I contacted you only by What's App and did not arrange any visits. We never felt safe. The

house had a wall around it and a guard with a dog, day and night. At first we stayed in, watching the

sea in its many moods, learning about each other, reading, listening to music. Then, as weeks passed and nothing happened we became bolder and started to explore the area, eating out, swimming in

the coves, enjoying life again. Then COVID happened. I think we caught it from our cleaner who

worked for many people in the area. She rang to say that she had a cough so was not coming, but

she'd been in our house a few days earlier. Andrei felt ill first, with chills and fever, plus a cough. We

called a doctor, who said that as Andrei could not smell or taste anything then it was highly likely to

be COVID-19. We should rest, take painkillers, drink plenty of fluids. That we did but after nearly a

week Andrei was worse- he looked grey, was sweaty and having trouble breathing. I called the doctor

again – he didn't bother to come, just told me to take Andrei straight to hospital in Paphos. It was a

nightmare journey, Andrei was gasping, and I was trembling so much it was hard to drive- but we got there and the staff were great. One look at him and they swung into action, giving him oxygen,

putting up a drip, getting his chest X rayed and blood tests and COVID swabs done. I was determined

to stay close to him, so said I has similar symptoms, which was true- but mine were much milder.

They took a swab from my nose and throat, but said that as I was not ill enough to admit I should go

home and keep in touch by phone. It was awful, leaving him there, but I could see that I was just in

the way- so I left. We kept in touch using mobiles- his had to be held in front of his face by a nurse- so

there wasn't much we could say. After 3 long days and nights he seemed to be improving and I began

to hope. Then in the middle of the next night the hospital rang and asked me to get there very fast,

Andrei had suddenly gone downhill. I was trembling, half asleep and I managed to hit another car on the way there- I rear ended him when he stopped at a red light. He was very cross to begin with,

"You stupid woman, what are you playing at?"

I burst into tears and sobbed out.

"My husband is dying; I have to get to the hospital."

Then he calmed down, helped me move my car to the side and took me to the hospital in his- which was less damaged. We exchanged details on the way there.

I was with Andrei at the end. He was just conscious, knew it was me, smiled. I held his hand, they

wouldn't let me hug or kiss him, until I remembered my test. Someone checked it out- positive- so

then I took off my mask and put my face next to his cheek, giving him the little gentle kisses that he

loved on the only part of his face outside the mask. He wasn't on a ventilator- I found out later they

take the dying people off them, perhaps because they didn't have enough for everyone who needed them. At the time I was glad because then he'd have been sedated and would not have known I was

there, now I wonder if it would have made a difference, could it have saved him to be ventilated for

longer? Anyway it was gentle and calm, a very beautiful time between us...."

Ti had tears running down her cheeks, for a moment she was unable to go on.

"Aaah, I have to get through this quickly. Sorry love."

"I am so sorry for you. What happened then?"

Ti straightened her back and went on

"Andrei died. There were forms to fill in- while bending forward doing them I found my neck had

locked as if in a vice and I couldn't use my arms and hands properly. I told the nurse and explained

about the car accident. She got a doctor who thought I might have damaged my neck in the car

crash. He said that I needed an Xray- which wasn't good because there was no way of getting one that night- the machine had broken and needed repair. The safest thing was to admit me and keep

my neck still. So they put me a collar and gave me some painkillers. I had to share a room- when I

told them I'd had a COVID test there recently they checked the result, found it was positive, so I was

sent to the COVID ward and put into a side room with one other bed in it. I tried to ring you, but

couldn't get through, so I left a message then cried myself to sleep."

"You poor love," I gave her a hug, awkwardly sideways because of the confined space in the Landy.

"It gets worse. Next day I woke early, the woman in the next bed was grey, not breathing, dead. I

was about to ring for a nurse when a thought struck me. In the first days when we were at home with

COVID Andrei opened up to me. He knew that his chances were not good. The gas story was true, but there was something else. He had secreted a small box in a safe deposit in a bank we used in

Limassol. If he died, I was to retrieve it as soon as possible. The contents included a USB with codes for

a small fortune in bitcoin and evidence of Putin's possession of a secret mega villa and of his

involvement in several high- profile murders- you remember Boris, his former friend?"

I nodded; I had read of Boris Berezovsky's untimely death. A coroner has recorded an open verdict:

the police pathologist said he could rule out murder, but one retained by the family found wounds

incompatible with suicide and suggested that Berezovsky had been murdered and then hung up.

"That was Andrei's insurance policy- he'd let Putin's underlings know that he'd arranged for the

details to be made public if he died. But he hadn't worked out the best way to do that. He knew that I had M16 connections, he'd realized from the start. That's why he asked me for a drink in the first

place."

"Oh no- so it wasn't love at first sight?"

"Not for him, apparently. It certainly was for me. But he did love me, I am sure of that. Why would he

have bothered to marry me otherwise?"

I thought privately that there might have been other reasons such as a British passport, but had the

sense not to say so.

"Andrei thought that I could arrange for the contents to be made public if he died under mysterious

circumstances, but he'd not wanted me to have access while he was fine- in case I felt duty bound to

pass them to M16 and he lost his insurance policy."

"Would you have done that?"

"No, of course not. I loved him too much to sell him out- even for the good of disgracing Putin."

"Now that his demise was a possibility, he wanted me to have access to the box. I was not to take it

unless he died. He gave me the key for the container in the bank and the code for opening the USB. I

had to memorize it, so I did."

Ti had always had a superb memory, as I knew from Kim's game, which we played on wet miserable

days.

"The only problem would be that if the Russians found out that he'd died in Cyprus – from natural

causes- they would wait to see if the facts came out. If not, they would assume the box had passed to

me, as his wife. That made me a target."

"Oh, hell! That's why you've been hiding away."

"Yes. I realized the problem that morning and did something awful- swapped identities with the dead

woman. She looked quite like me, about the same age, similar colouring, same length hair. It was not hard, I just switched our lockers round, moved the chart from my bed to hers and vice versa – and

walked out with her handbag and a bag of possessions, taking my own passport, phone and driving

licence from mine too. Even though I couldn't use them I did not want them to fall into the wrong

hands. It was believable that in my haste to reach Andrei I had left them at home. My clothes I left in

the locker, credit and debit cards stayed in the handbag that I left behind. I even put the neck support

onto her- it was just a horrible thing to do, but I told myself that she would not mind, being dead."

"Ugh."

I knew that the staff would exchange information at the desk before the new lot came round – so

they'd hear about me being admitted with a neck injury. I just had to hope that they buy into it

proving suddenly fatal- but that was why I'd been admitted, in case I had an unstable neck fracture.

There'd have to be a post- mortem- there were big delays with those, so but by the time that

happened I'd be away and in hiding."

"Then I went to the loo, changed into her clothes, fortunately she was slightly bigger than me so no

problem getting into them- and let myself out of the ward when no- one was looking. I didn't dare

use the lift so used the back stairs and came out of a service entrance. It was still early so no- one

was around. I tried to look as though I'd just finished a night's work- fiddled in the handbag and

found a set of car keys. It's wonderful these days- all you do is press the remote and the relevant car

beeps. Nothing happened when I did it. My heart sank- there was not much money in the bag, I

should have removed some of my own but did not dare go back inside. Then I realized that I was in

the staff car park- so I walked confidently round to the other one, pressed the remote again- and found the car. I let out my breath which I'd been holding for ages, climbed in and tried to start it.

Nothing. Then I remembered our hire car- where you have to put the clutch right in before turning

the key. It started. I was away in a little Suzuki."

"Wouldn't the staff wonder where she'd gone?"

"Yes, but with luck they'd think she'd absconded. They were worked off their feet by COVID with no

time for anything extra. I guessed they'd let the police know once they found out so I couldn't keep

the car long. At first, I drove towards our Sea Caves house, but after a couple of miles realized that I'd

left the keys to it behind in my handbag and in any case it might be watched, so I turned the car and

drove back the way I'd come from. I thought about going to the airport, but had no money for a

ticket or for car hire, no cards and I didn't dare use her card because big amounts meant I'd need the code and I didn't know it. I had switched my phone off so as not to be traced. What to do? I

wondered about trying to go back to the ward and pretending to be her- but I don't speak Greek, so

that deception wouldn't have lasted long. By this time, I'd driven through Paphos and onto the

motorway. A sign said Lefkosia- and suddenly the idea came to me. I'd go to the one person in Cyprus

whom I knew."

Ti looked at me.

"Can't you guess?"

I shook my head,

"Costas, you picked him up in Queen's Park years ago, when you'd run away. Don't you remember?"

I laughed, "Of course, lovely Costas- he kept coming round after that."

"To see me, "Ti said.

"Oh." I had rather thought that it was me he came to play with.

"We went out for a while, without saying anything to your M&D."

"Oh."

"Anyway, I knew his address in Nicosia – so I drove there, just enough petrol in the Suzuki to reach the

city and abandon it in an underground car park. Then I took a taxi to Costas' address. It was still only

8 am so he was there and very pleased to see me. I asked if I could come in. Fortunately, he lives

alone, so that was fine. He made me coffee and I just sat down and burst into tears. My neck hurt, I

was scared and unsure of what to do. Costas was great- he had to go to work- so suggested I had a

sleep, ate something when I felt like it then we could talk when he returned that evening. I made him

promise to say nothing about me to anyone. He looked surprised but agreed."

CHAPTER 14

Ti looked at her watch.

"We are running out of time. The reason I had to see you
was to warn you."

"Warn me? What about?"

"I didn't collect the deposit box- I couldn't because that
would have meant using Andrei's death

certificate to gain probate- and I was supposedly dead too.
It is still there- and now it belongs to

you."

"Me?"

"Yes, when we married Andrei said we needed to make
our wills again as our circumstances had

changed. We did it in Paphos at a lawyer called Antoniades.
If I died Andrei was to have all I owned,

if he predeceased me," Ti paused, looked down, then went
on, " then I left everything to you

sweetheart. I thought I was doing you a favour, but in fact you are now about to become a multi-

millionairess with access to secrets and a price on your head. I am so sorry."

My mind refused to function- or rather it was darting off in several directions at once.

"I have to go to that lawyer while we're here. What should I do?"

"Go soon, but don't take Nick. Don't tell him anything, please."

"What?" I was immediately furious," Nick has nothing to do with all this."

Ti made a placatory gesture with her hands, "That is likely, but just in case, please go alone. Accept

the bequest with surprise, it will include the Sea Caves house. Once you have probate then hot foot

it to the bank, get the contents and meet me nearby. We can send the secret stuff to Dad. He'll

know what to do with it. "

"OK."

"I'll send you the details of the bank and the code, separately. Please give me your phone."

I passed it over and she put in a number under the name Beatrice Epstein.

"I was at school with her," I said.

"That's why I've used that name – you'll remember it is me- and no- one will think it odd for you to

have her number. We can be in touch now via Signal. It is safer than What's App these days."

Ti looked out of the windows, gazing all around. No- one was in view.

"OK, I'll drive you back to near Turtle Beach, then you can walk from there.   Please get in the back

and slip down again so you can't be seen."

I was silent while crouched down uncomfortably in the back of the Landy. Life had just taken a big

turn for the worse. What worried me most was that Ti obviously thought Nick might be mixed up in it. That made me want to hate her, for the first time ever.

We parted hastily, with me slipping out of the rear side door, crouched low, then running down to

the beach and sitting down there before Ti drove off- so it did not look as though I'd been in the

Landy. That was her idea- I went along with it, feeling remarkably silly. When she'd gone I stood up,

brushed sand from my backside and began the long walk back up to the car and Nick. My brain

refused to get into gear, just kept grinding the clutch of an idea that Ti had planted. Was Nick

involved?

They say that walking is good for thought- in the end it did seem that way. The steady climb and the

rhythm of my feet allowed me to formulate a plan of sorts- I would, as Ti had asked, say nothing to

Nick, but would watch him, like the proverbial hawk- or Griffon vulture.

He was sitting in the car, reading the guidebook I'd left in there. He saw me and smiled, got out and

came and gave me a hug, then bent his face to mine for a kiss.

"How about a PDA? I've missed you."

"I've missed you too." That was easy enough to say, and I meant it.

"How did you get into the car?"

"You left the keys in the door, fortunately no- one nicked it"

That must have been when I saw Ti, I thought.

"Oh sugar, I am so sorry."

"Didn't matter" as it happened. Please don't make a habit of it."

Nick then explained that he'd had to give up trying to reach the top end of the gorge as it was

blocked by piles of rubble, so he'd returned to the car and had been waiting a while.

"You were sensible to go back. It just became more and more difficult."

"Good."

Lying does not come easily to me, I did not want to fabricate a story about the Turtle Beach.

"Let's go home. I'm tired." That was true, Ti's story had made me feel exhausted.

"Sure."

Nick drove us back to our little sunny apartment where I made us a salad. We balcony- sat (an

expression that had come into use as it was a frequent activity) to eat and watched the sun sparkling

 on the sea. Nick leaned across the table to reach my hand and hold it. Being with him again

reassured me.

"He loves me, he really loves me," I thought.

"Let's swim when this food has gone down," Nick suggested. "Come down to the cove below the house with me. It's a bit of a scramble, but the sea is calm today and it's a good place to snorkel. The

sun makes it warm in late afternoon too."

We did. I took a book and after a short swim I lay on a rock reading, while Nick stayed in the water,

going in and out of the sea caves that gave the area its name: Thalassines spilies. He was hoping to

see a monk seal, which are said to breed in the caves, but failed. He was right about the sun though,

it warmed the cove beautifully and I began to feel wonderfully relaxed and sleepy. My mind

wandered, but returned to Ti. How had she managed to get to my wedding? Was it her voice I'd

heard by the swimming pool a few days ago? Where was she staying now?

My phone chirruped, startling me back to wakefulness. It was a message from my mother, asking

about the solicitor.

"Had I seen Mr Antoniades yet?"

I replied" No, will do soon."

Then I began to wonder what my mother knew. Did she know Ti was alive? I had to talk to Ti again

soon. I sent a message to Beatrice Epstein,

"When is good for Mr A?"

A rapid reply appeared.

"ASAP."

The reception for a phone call was poor down in the cove.

"Nick, I am going to go back to the flat," I called.

His head with its snorkel pipe continued to move through the sea, propelled by flippered feet. I set

off scrambling up the path to the cliff top, paused there to catch my breath and yelled down again to

let Nick know. He continued swimming. I decided to go home, make the call, then return.

The two big windows giving onto the balcony were visible on my way up. I glanced at them, blinked, glanced again. It looked as though there was someone in our flat, in our bedroom. I stopped, unsure

of what to do, then decided that discretion was the better part of valour and raced back down to the

cove.

"Nick, Nick, "I was calling as I ran. This time he heard and swam to the rocky shore in time to meet

me on my slide downhill towards it.

"What's up?" he asked.

I was panting, partly from exertion, partly fear.

"There's someone in the flat. I could see them in the window."

"Are you sure, love? Perhaps it was just a shadow."

"No, I think it was a person. Please come with me."

"Of course. Just let me dry my feet and put shoes on."

Nick took what seemed like a long time to carefully dry between each toe before slipping on his sandals. Then he led the way back up the slope, carefully and not fast. I followed, wanting to hurry,

but felt constrained from saying so in case he was scared too. At the top our view of the windows

was initially blocked by trees, but once beyond them the balcony and both windows were easily

visible. No- one was there, at least there was no shadow in either window.

Nick squeezed my hand which he'd been holding since we reached the top, then let it go and put his

arm around my shoulders.

"Looks OK to me, love. Let's go in."

We climbed up the steps through the garden, used our key to open the back door of our block, and

entered. All was quiet. Nick turned to me and put his finger to his lips. I nodded. We crept upstairs to

our flat's closed front door and stood outside, listening intently. Nothing. Nick pushed me gently behind him, then inserted his key into the lock and turned it slightly, pushing the door open rapidly.

The lobby was empty, so was the kitchen. He turned into the bedroom- no- one was there.

Meanwhile I had entered the sitting room, which was also empty. We met in the kitchen.

"Sweetheart, I think you have a vivid imagination."

"Sorry, I really thought I saw someone. Thanks for coming back with me."

"No problem. It's getting cooler so let's shower and go out for some supper."

"Good idea. You go first, you're shivering."

While Nick was in the shower, I made the phone call to Mr Antoniades and arranged an appointment

for the day after next. I looked for my handbag to make a note in my diary, but it was not where I'd

left it under my pillow. That was strange- it was one of my ingrained habits to hide my handbag under my pillow whenever I left any house without it. I searched the room, finding no sign of it in the

wardrobe or any of the drawers. Finally, I got down on my knees to check all the floor and found it,

 unzipped, under the bed. My arm was just long enough to reach it and I hauled it towards me,

bringing some underbed fluff with it. Riffling through it nothing appeared to be missing, my wallet

with its euros and cards was still there, my diary, together with lipstick, tissues, the many things I

carry around with me. For a moment I wondered if I'd left it like that- but knew that I had not. There

had been someone in the flat. Someone who'd left in a hurry, perhaps when he (she?) had seen us

returning. It would have been easy to leave fast by the front door of the block, even as we entered

by the back, one floor below.

Nick entered the room, clad in a towel round his waist, another rubbing his head.

"Sorry to take so long, but the shower only dribbles, took me ages to get the shampoo off my hair."

I glanced up at him from my perch on the bed.

"No problem. It's the limescale that clogs everything up. But someone was here."

"How do you know?"

"My handbag was open, under the bed."

"Anything missing?"

"I don't think so, perhaps we scared him off."

"I'll check my stuff."

It didn't take long, nothing was gone.

"What should we do?"

Nick thought for a moment, then suggested,

"I'll contact the host via Airbnb- perhaps we can get the locks changed."

"OK- but I don't want to go out again tonight and leave the place empty. I'd rather stay here, double locking the door and putting a tilted chair against it."

"Sure, do we have enough food?"

"Yes, I can make us spaghetti with tomato sauce and more salad. We have a bottle of red under the

sink."

The large undersink cupboard was the coolest place in the flat and did as our root vegetable store

and wine cellar as well as housing the cleaning stuff and cloths.

Nick did as he promised, and the host agreed that we should change the locks at his expense. He

gave us the name and number of a local man who would do the job quickly. Meanwhile I produced

our supper and we ate as usual on the balcony, at a candlelit table surrounded by a blackness of sea

and sky with little distinction between them. Occasional lights of fishing boats could be seen in the

distance and then an array of lights, probably denoting a cruise ship, much further out. Straining our ears we could just make out the strains of music coming from it. Suddenly it disappeared.

"Fell off the edge of the world, I think, "laughed Nick.

I smiled, but the ship reminded me of Ti and of the problems that I now had to face.

CHAPTER 15

For the first time since arriving in Cyprus we did not make love that night.

Nick made an attempt to stroke me, but I turned my head away and said,

"Not tonight, Josephine. Sorry, I am bushwhacked."

He laughed, then kissed me on the forehead and turned away, settling down to sleep. I tried to do the same but found my brain too active and full of questions.

Was Ti safe? Did Andrei really love her? What actually was on the USB?

Was I safe? What about Nick? Was he innocent? Did he know anything about the USB? Who was in

our flat?

Did my Mum know Ti was alive?

Eventually I gave up trying to sleep, slipped out of bed and onto the balcony, where I sat, knees

drawn up to my chin, looking at the stars. As always, they made me feel small and insignificant, my worries infinitesimal against the backdrop of an infinite universe. I recited in my head chants and

prayers that I'd learnt during my course and felt my heartbeat slowing, my mind settling. I returned

quietly to bed and to sleep.

Next day again dawned bright and clear. We had to stay home because Nick had managed to contact

the local locksmith who was coming at 11am. I sat reading on the balcony and became too hot.

"Why don't you have a swim in the pool love?" Nick said. "I can hold the fort here."

So I did. Having taken my phone with me I slipped into one of the alcoves invisible from out flat and

sent a message to Beatrice Epstein about the time I'd arranged for my meeting with the solicitor.

"Mr A, 11am tomorrow."

She knew the whereabouts of the office having done her will there. I looked it up on Google maps-

and worked out how to drive to it and where to park. I sent a second message simply saying "Car"

and the car park co- ordinates, so she could find me there if she wished. Once sent I wiped them

from the phone memory congratulating myself on my espionage tactics derived from books.

Then I enjoyed a swim, my usual 40 lengths plus some exercises. It is such a pleasure to exercise in

water and not get hot and sweaty. My body is well-adapted to the aquatic life and

consequently I love spending time in the water, provided I can keep my ears dry.

Nick called down to say the locksmith had arrived, so I climbed out, dried myself quickly and went up

to meet him. Nick asked if anyone had interfered with the locks- he thought not, said there were no

marks to indicate that- so whoever was in our flat had a key. Well that key would soon be useless.

That was a comfort. When the locks had been changed, we'd given the locksmith a cup of coffee and

paid him in cash, he left and Nick and I were alone again.

"What do you fancy doing today?" Nick asked.

"How about we walk along the cliffs? Perhaps we can bathe further along?"

"Sure, I'll get my stuff."

Since I was already in a swimsuit I spent a few minutes putting together a small picnic and filling the

rucksack with it, water, and towels. Then I slipped on a T-shirt and shorts, and we were ready to go.

"Let's take one set of the new keys and hide the other one somewhere in here. How about in the

washing machine?"

"Great, as long as we don't forget and run it with them inside."

The cliff walk began at the end of the posh houses set in quiet to the right of our block as you faced the sea. We strolled past them, gazing at the massive staircases, carefully landscaped gardens, pools,

jacuzzis, trampolines, solar panels with which abounded in their gardens. Each had a Beware of the

Dog notice. That reminded me of Ti and Andrei- was it in one of these that they'd lived? Was one of

these part of my inheritance?

The walk was beautiful at first, over chalk cliffs hollowed and sculpted by years of sea contact into

ridges, whorls, caves, outlying rocks. I kept stopping to take photos on my phone, loving the multiple

sparkling reflections of the sun upon the waves. Nick humoured me, taking the rucksack to make it

easier for me to use the phone camera. After a quarter of a mile there was a low flat building on the

horizon, looking a little like a prison, for it had slits instead of windows in the side facing us. As we

approached it turned into a modern house, accompanied by many more of the same, all designed with that "tunnel vision" beloved of modern Cypriot architects. The same look could have been

achieved by using shipping containers, one upon another. Although the landscaping was good, with

lots of trees and shrubs, the overall effect was entirely depressing: a large housing estate built in a

lovely place which had until then been wild and home to wildlife such as endangered monk seals.

"How could anyone allow this?" I asked.

"Money" said Nick. "Pay enough to the right people and you get what you want in this country."

"But they will not last", I said. "Look at that island out there, the side has clearly fallen away recently,

you can tell by the white scar. The same will happen here and the houses will fall into the sea."

"Not before someone has made a big profit out of them."

"That's awful."

"Yes, it is, but Cyprus was broke in 2012. The golden passport scheme allowed the country to make money- which has been spent, at least in part, on improving the lives of its citizens. Is that so bad?"

I looked him straight in the eye.

"Yes, if it destroys the environment and the beauty of the island. Cyprus is selling its birth right for a

mess of pottage."

Nick looked thoughtful. He was quiet for a moment, then spoke.

"You are right. I am usually so proud to be a son of Cypriot parents, but sometimes I am ashamed by

my country."

His usually cheerful face looked downcast. I reached for his hand and squeezed it gently.

"We can all do better in future."

As we had been walking the sky had darkened in the north and large clouds were scudding towards

us. They blotted out the warm sunshine. It was amazing how quickly the scene had changed from bright, cheerful sunshine to threatening darkness. With my still damp swimsuit next to my skin I

began to shiver. Thunder rolled in the distance.

"Let's go home."

Nick looked at me and understood.

"OK"

We turned round and hurried back along the undulating, twisting path, reaching the made road just

as the first large drops of rain began to fall.

"Race you!"

I knew he'd win, but also that winning would please him. Men are so simple.

He'd left the back door to Block A open for me. Puffing from the run and the climb up the garden

steps, I passed gratefully through it into dryness, but no warmth. By the time I entered the flat Nick

had already put on the immersion heater and was towelling his wet head and shoulders.

"Come here."

He lifted the towel over my head and began rubbing my hair vigorously.

"Let's see if there's enough hot water for a bath."

There was.

CHAPTER 16.

"Watch the speed limits. Another way that Cyprus makes money is from speeding fines. "

Nick had noticed the illuminated headlights of approaching cars.

I slowed down to the requisite 50mph, just in time to be legal for the speed trap radar gun that the

yellow jacketed policeman was pointing at us.

We were on our way to Paphos for my legal appointment. I was nervous and therefore driving fast.

Nick was not going into the lawyer's office with me but had asked me to drop him at the Kings Mall

on my way as he had a few things he needed to buy. That part of the journey was simple. I found the

mall, swerved into the underground car park and let Nick out.

"Let's meet right here in 2 hours," I suggested. "If I'm going to be late I'll ring you."

"Sure, good luck love. Hope it goes well." He leaned across and kissed me, then got out of the car

and walked away towards the lift, not looking back.

I was afraid of getting lost, despite the sat nav. and had almost asked Nick to come with me as far as

the lawyer's office. That would have made it difficult to meet Ti – so I hadn't asked and now just had

to do my best. The first hurdle was getting out of the car park- I had to pay, even though I had spent

only minutes inside the mall car park. That meant finding a machine, inserting the ticket I'd picked

up on entering and paying the cost. Of course, I did not have the right change so ended up using my

credit card, doubtless at added expense. By the time I'd exited through the barrier, having inserted

the paid for ticket- which I'd forgotten in the machine and had to go back for- I was sweaty and

anxious. In fact the journey was fairly easy and within 10 minutes I had located the car park whose co- ordinates I'd transmitted to Ti. There was no machine, no mention of payment. I just picked up

my handbag, which Nick insisted on calling my reticule, locked the car and set off on foot the short

distance to Antoniades and Discorides, Attorneys at Law.

The office was in a modern block, with numerous entry phones on the wall outside the imposing

double doors. I pressed the relevant one and was greeted by a female voice,

"Antoniades and Discorides, do you have an appointment?"

On informing her that I did she invited me to enter and take the lift to the top floor, so I did just that.

The glass doors to an office opened into the small hallway opposite the lift. On either side of the hall

were more wooden doors. Through the glass I could see a young woman, dark- haired, handsome

rather than pretty, with a strong face and a hooked nose, getting up from a desk. She opened the

glass door and greeted me,

"Chloe de Sanges?"

"Yes." I was actually Chloe Nicolaou now, but that fact had not caught up with me yet. I still

responded to my maiden name- and that was the one on my current passport.

"Mr Antoniades is still with a client. Would you mind waiting for a few minutes?"

"Sure, that's no problem. I think I am early anyway. "

The girl opened one of the wooden doors and showed me into a small waiting room with a

wonderful view over Paphos to the sea beyond.

"What a glorious view!"

"Yes," she said, nearly as good as yours at Sea Caves, I think."

I nodded, trying not to show how startled I was. How did she know about Sea Caves? I had said

nothing of my whereabouts on the phone when I made the appointment.

"Please could I have your passport briefly? I need to take a photocopy."

She left me alone, shutting the door behind her. I racked my brains- had I mentioned Sea Caves at

all? No, I was sure not. Perhaps my mother had when dealing with them. Did she know we had a

great view? I may have told her, but would she have bothered to pass that on to the lawyer's

secretary?

The secretary returned, gave me back my passport and asked me to follow her. I was led to a door

opposite, she knocked on it and entered.

"Chloe de Sanges," she announced.

"Do come in Miss de Sanges. Allow me to introduce myself, Demetrios Antoniades."

He was middle- aged, overweight, handsome in a florid fashion with wavy greying hair brushed back

from his face. Instantly I distrusted him.

He held out a hand which I shook.

"Do sit down."

I did. I felt scared and wished that I were not alone.

Mr Antoniades commiserated with me on the loss of my aunt at such a young age. It was such a pity

that fate in the form of COVID had dealt her and her husband such awful blows. He told me of their

visit to him, Felicity and Andrei, and how they had made wills together just in case of disaster. He

commended their foresight and suggested that I should lose no time in making my own will once he

had dealt with the business of today. Then he opened the folder on his desk and explained that since

Andrei had died first all his possessions passed to Felicity, then on her untimely death everything

was to be distributed according to her wishes. He then read out Ti's last will and testament. It

nearly provoked tears to hear her words, "to my beloved niece Chloe de Sanges.." and would have done, had I not seen her in the flesh a few days before. Everything of hers was left to me,

unconditionally. There was a house at Sea Caves-"a very classy area, you know"-plus bank accounts

and deposits. He droned on.

Sea Caves- perhaps the will was where the secretary had it from. She'd probably typed it up. But

wasn't it a bit unprofessional to mention something in the will that I was about to hear?

There was silence. Mr A had stopped talking. I gave a tentative smile and asked what I needed to do

next. Apparently, I had to sign several documents, pay the firm for what they had done in rescuing

Ti's possessions from the hospital and storing them and in keeping the house clean and a guard

employed, then I could leave with them and with details of the bank accounts et cetera. Before I did

so he strongly advised me to consider making a will of my own very soon, since I now possessed considerable assets.

I thanked him, he pressed a buzzer, and the secretary came in bearing more papers. I read them

quickly, signed them and she witnessed my signature. Her name was Sophia Nicolaou.

Although I longed to ask her if she knew Nick, if she was a relative, I said nothing. Perhaps at some

level I did not want to know. Gathering up the papers and handbag I left, giving a sigh of relief in the

lift. I had done what Ti asked, now she could take over. Hurrying back to the car park I half- noticed

a young man apparently mending a bicycle puncture outside the office block. Ti was not in the car

park, nor was the Landy. Getting into the Suzuki I saw that young man, now minus bicycle, strolling

past the entrance. Was I being watched? The thought sent shivers down my spine. I wished I'd had

Ti's spy training. Minutes ticked by and I continued to wait, sweating a little in the small car, heart ticking over quickly.

CHAPTER 17.

Suddenly there was a rap on the passenger window, by a disembodied hand. I leaned over the gear

stick and saw the top of Ti's head, with the same dark wig. She must be crouched there beside the

car. I unlocked that door, pushing it a little way open. Ti asked me to open the rear door, then

squeezed in, keeping low on the vehicle floor.

"Drive off Chloe love, let's go to Limassol and that bank."

"Ti, I can't, I have to pick Nick up soon."

"Drive anyway, we can talk while you do. How did you get on?"

"Mr A told me all about your visit and the will, then I had to sign lots of papers- I've got copies of all

of them- and pay them."

"For what?"

"For looking after the stuff you left in the hospital and for the house protection."

"OK."

"Did he give you my handbag?"

"Yes, it's here."

I moved it from the footwell and deposited it on the back seat. Ti took it and peered inside.

"The keys to the house are here."

Then later, "Everything is still there."

While this was going on I had been driving, going back in the direction of the Kings Mall, more or less

on autopilot to lose any possible surveillance. There was no sign of bicycle boy and as far as I could

tell no car following us. But I could hardly pickup Nick with Ti in the car. I told Ti and asked her what

we should do now.

"Best thing would be to get to Limassol asap, go to the bank, get that USB and send the contents to

Dad. You did bring your computer as I asked?"

"Yes, it's in the boot."

"OK, turn round when you can and take the motorway. What time did you say to Nick?"

"Two hours, it's been just over one so far."

"We can get to Limassol in under an hour, then you can ring him from there and say you've been

delayed. He can take a taxi home."

"Only one problem", I found myself saying.

"What's that?"

"Mr A's secretary has the same surname as Nick, and she knew we were staying at Sea Caves. I

hadn't told her- so I wonder if Nick had?"

Ti was quiet for a minute. Then she said,

"If they are connected then Nick knows what is going on. The secretary will have typed up our wills

and will know about the Limassol bank account. Sweetheart, how about for the time being we put

Nick into the Bad Guy category? I'm not saying he definitely is and that decision is open to change, but for now, it is the safest thing to do. It also means that we must go straight to the Limassol bank

now. I am very sorry because you obviously care deeply for him…"

"Shut up." I'd not spoken like that to Ti for many years." I need to concentrate on driving right now."

"OK."

I took the car all the way round the big roundabout by the mall and then a quarter way round again

in order to reach the motorway.

"Nice one sweetheart, is anyone following us?"

"It was accidental, I missed it the first time, but, no, I don't think we are being tailed."

We travelled eastwards along the motorway in silence, both busy with our thoughts. I could not

believe Nick was a Bad Guy, I was sure that his love for me was genuine but had no way to prove

that to Ti. Perhaps Sophia's surname was a coincidence. Nicolaou was probably an incredibly common name in Cyprus. I wished that he was in the car with us and could tell both of us the truth.

Signs for Limassol began to appear.

"Which Exodus do we need?"

She laughed.

"The bank is on the far side of Limassol, near where we were staying, take no 21 and I'll direct you

from there."

I did that and within 45 minutes I was stopping the car near the Bank of Cyprus.

"Sorry Chloe you are going to have to go it alone again. They have seen me before in this bank – so I

dare not come in with you, even in this disguise, just in case someone recognises me. What you need

to do is to introduce yourself, show them your passport and the will and probate documents and ask

them to take you to the deposit box. It's in a basement place with lots of others- they'll bring the box to you. Here is the key."

She removed it from a chain around her neck and gave it to me.

"Bring out all the contents, including the USB, but put something back into the box and lock it for

them to store. Then come out and I'll be waiting here in the car. Ring me if you have any problems."

"If you tell me the code, I can copy everything from the USB onto my computer, then leave the USB

safely in the box."

"I don't know how much stuff is on it, nor how long transferring it will take. Also, I'd like to move the

USB to a different hiding place- so just bring it out please love."

"It makes sense to make an immediate copy Ti, you know that."

"OK, here is the code. Learn it please."

She wrote it on a page from a notebook she had in her handbag and showed it to me. I studied it carefully, wrote it again on the paper, having folded the top down so I could not see it, checked it,

did the same twice more- correct each time.

"Got it. "

Ti put the paper into her mouth and chewed it carefully before swallowing it.

I entered the bank, carrying my rucksack with the computer in it. There were a couple of people

queueing for a teller. I looked around and found another desk with a man seated at it. I decided to

try him. It is hard to look authoritative if you are short, even harder when carrying a rucksack. With

my back straight I walked up to him and said,

"Good morning, I'd like to see my safety deposit box please."

He looked gloomy.

"It is nearly the time when we close. Please come back tomorrow."

"I am sorry, but it is urgent. It will not take long. Here are my documents and my passport."

Looking fierce, I gave him the probate document and my passport.

He took them, with a sigh. After a rapid perusal he checked my face and the passport photo, then

logged into his computer. It took a while for him to find what he was looking for, then he said,

"Follow me please."

I did. We went through a door protected by a key code, into a lift and down to the basement. There

another code protected door was opened and we were in a room with multiple small, locked doors

all around the walls, a bit like a luggage office, only smaller. The man unlocked one of them and

handed me a rectangular black metal box, also locked.

"You have the key? "

"Yes, thank you."

"Good. I will leave you here. Please ring this buzzer when you want to be let out. Will you be all

right?"

I nodded, feeling somewhat scared and claustrophobic, but determined to do this right for Ti.

The man departed. As soon as the door closed behind him I inserted the key into the box, turned it

and opened the lid.

There were several things inside: papers, a small jewellery box, some photographs, a couple of

passports. No USB. I checked and re- checked. No USB.

I was trembling and sweating, partly from fear, partly from anger.

"Bloody Andrei, "I said out loud, letting some of my anger at Nick's possible treachery spill over onto

Ti's lover.

"What did you really do with it? Does it even exist?"

The papers were in Russian, which I cannot read or speak. Ti would be able to read them though, so I

put them into my rucksack, with the photos and passports and deposited a few of my notes on

Cyprus in the box instead.

Finally, I thought to open the little jewel case- of course the USB was inside it. Cursing my stupidity, I

quickly turned on my computer and inserted the USB drive. A window opened with more Russian

characters. There was a blank area, so I typed the code in there and clicked on the green part below

 it. There was a pause then it opened to reveal a mass of headings, all in Russian. I copied them one

by one to my hard drive, it took several minutes for the first one, the second was even longer and

halfway through it I began to wonder if the bank would close leaving me stuck down there until the

next day. I began to panic, to feel claustrophobic. I had to get out of there. There was no way I could copy everything on it before leaving, so I closed the USB and slipped it into my bra, closed the

computer and put the empty jewel case back into the safe deposit box, locked it and pressed the exit

buzzer. It took several anxious minutes before the door opened and I was allowed out, clutching my

rucksack with computer safely inside.

CHAPTER 18

"How did you get on?" asked Ti when I reached the car.

"Semi OK, there was too much stuff to put all of it onto my computer. I've got the USB though. "

"Great, well done Chloe. I'll take us somewhere safe where we can check what's on it and you can

pass it to Dad. He'll know what to do with it."

"OK, I must ring Nick- it's after the time I should have picked him up." I pressed Nick's name on my

mobile.

"Hi Chloe, where are you?"

I am a hopeless liar, so avoided that issue completely by saying,

"Sorry my darling, I've been held up with stuff about the will. Please take a taxi home and I'll join you

when I can."

"No worries, I can amuse myself here a bit longer. How long do you think you'll be?"

"I don't know love. It could take a while. You make your own arrangements and I'll see you back at

home."

"Is there a problem with the will?"

"Complications, yes. See you later love." I ended the call and switched off my phone. I wanted to

believe Nick was on the side of the angels, but Ms Nicolaou had dented my certainty about that.

"Where are we going?"

I asked Ti, who was now driving the little car, presumably uninsured, because how could you insure

a dead person?

"To see a friend of yours."

We took the motorway signed Lefkosia, which I now knew meant Nicosia. On the way Ti told me

more of what had happened to her. Costas had sheltered her until she'd managed to get a message

to her M16 handler. Then she had been given a new identity, clothing and a back story to match. At

first she lived in Nicosia, doing translation work from Russian to English, mainly for the UK diplomatic

service. MI6 were biding time, waiting to ensure that the story of her death would be verified by the

Cypriot authorities, then accepted by Putin's pals. When she heard from Costas that he'd had an

invitation to my forthcoming wedding to someone with a Greek name she determined to be there,

even though she knew her disguise would not fool any of the family. Ti was worried that somehow

Nick had found out that I was likely to inherit a fortune, once Ti's death was accepted. There was no way she could warn me without breaking cover and she was at risk from Putin's spies if they found

out she was alive. Costas was unable to attend- he could not get enough time off work- his wedding

gift with the legend, "Beware of Greeks bearing gifts" made more sense now.

Ti persuaded her handler to get her on a flight to the UK. Like so many flights in the COVID pandemic

it was cancelled late and she had to take the next one. Ti found herself arriving at Heathrow with

just enough time to catch the Express to Paddington and then the tube to near the church where the

wedding had already started. No way dare she enter the church, so she hid behind a gravestone to

watch me emerge as a married woman. That's when I saw her as she bobbed up to check whether

we were about to leave the ceremony.

She had fled the graveyard but returned when the wedding party had departed for the Reception, went into the church and said urgent prayers for me, Nick and our marriage. After that she set about

finding how to gain entrance to a University to repair the gaps in her education. No easy matter

when all her A and O level results were in her previous name.

Costas heard from my Mum that Nick had taken me to Cyprus for the honeymoon. He let Ti know

and she flew back to try to contact me, sort out the USB information and find out whether Nick was a good guy or not.

"I'll do the same as last time, park this car underground and we can take a taxi to Costas' flat."

Then after a pause,

"No, I think it's better if I drop you at his flat, watch you get in, then go and park the car. As soon as

you are with Costas ask him to let you use his computer. It's a powerful one with great internet as he

is a structural engineer and his work depends on it."

"Sure, but why don't we go to the Embassy here and hand it all to them?"

"Because I am not sure how far we can trust all of them. While I have been translating, I have come

 across some worrying stuff about contact with the regime in Russia. That was why MI6 got me in

there. Dad is a much safer bet. He knows that I am alive, but has told no- one, not even Mum."

"Poor Granny! She must be so sad to have lost you."

"Yes, I saw her at your wedding and thought how she'd aged. I felt terrible, responsible for that.

 When I made that snap decision to trade places the full impact did not occur to me until it was too

late to go back. It may have been the wrong thing to do, I don't know. If we can offload this Putin

stuff then the danger to both of us is past and I can reappear as myself. The first thing I'll do is to go

home and give my Mum a big hug and lots of kisses."

For the first time I realized the strain that Ti was under and felt sorry for her. Perhaps that was why

she was being so negative about Nick. I was sure that he was not involved in any spy malarkey.

Ti parked in the street outside a block of flats, then made a phone call while we remained in the car.

A large, familiar figure appeared in the doorway.

"OK Chloe, off you go. Take your rucksack, handbag, everything. Tell Costas I'll be along in minute-

but do get started on sending the stuff."

It was wonderful to see Costas again, after a gap of over ten years. He was just as I remembered

him: a big teddy bear of a man, with a warm smile and kind crinkly eyes.

"Chloe, oh Chloe, it is so good to see you."

He embraced me in a bear hug, more grizzly than teddy, on the doorstep.

"Please can we go inside, Costas?"

"Of course, I'd forgotten, Ti tells me that you have important things to do. Come along."

Costas led me to the lift and up to his floor, at the top of the building. His spacious, airy flat occupied

the whole top floor. He was obviously doing very well for himself.

"Here is my office."

Costas opened the door and ushered me in. There was a big computer screen on the desk, with a

screensaver picture of Queen's Park.

"Oh Costas, how lovely to see home. Did you take that picture?"

He nodded.

"My time in London was very special, your family was also very special to me, Chloe. It was a great

day when I met you."

"A great day for me too, Costas. Goodness knows what might have happened if you hadn't rescued me."

"It was nothing. Well of course it was something, something very special…."

His command of English failed him, so he covered up by pulling out the chair by the desktop- and

indicating that I should sit there. I did and had to adjust the chair height so that I could use the

keyboard. Costas logged in while I fiddled with the adjustment. Once I was settled, he asked,

"Do you need any help?"

"I don't think so, should I just call you if I do?"

"Sure." Taking the hint, Costas left the room, saying,

"I'll put the kettle on." That must have been a phrase he picked up in our house.

 Once he was gone, I was able to retrieve the USB from my bra and insert it into the computer stack.

Again, the password I'd memorized worked and the contents were available. I opened an e- mail to

Grandad's address, knowing it to be a secure diplomatic one, and proceeded to send him several e

mails, each with sections of the USB contents. It took a while. Costas brought me a cup of tea with

both milk and sugar. I hadn't the heart to tell him that I'd given up both.

"Is Ti here yet?"

"No, I don't know why it's taking her so long."

"Perhaps she can't find a taxi."

"I'll ring her. If she's stuck, I could go and collect her."

Costas took out his mobile and speed dialled a number. There was no reply. He tried again with the

same result.

"That's odd, Ti usually answers if it's me. I'll go round to the car park to check. You stay here Chloe."

He left the flat and I shivered, feeling scared for Ti and for myself. What had we got ourselves into?

I turned back to the computer and concentrated on getting the information from the USB to

Grandpa as fast as possible.

It was nearly an hour later when Costas returned with Ti. She looked pale and shaken. I rushed up to

her and gave her a hug.

"What happened?"

"Totally stupid stuff. I was walking out of the underground car park when a woman came up to me

asking directions to the old Turkish bath. I should have been more careful. I opened my phone to

show her – and she just snatched it and ran."

"You didn't catch her?" Ti had always been a good runner.

"No, there was a scooter waiting. A man in a helmet on the front. She hopped onto the back and off

they went."

"Do you think it was linked to the USB? What was on your phone?"

"I thought at first it might be linked, but the police have told me that this happens all the time, so I

think it is just straightforward crime. I just don't know though. I am trying hard to remember

everything that's on my phone- but it doesn't matter as it can all be blocked. It matters to me

though as I'll have to start again with contact numbers and all that, what a bugger!"

Amazingly Ti began to weep. I had never seen her like this. She sat on the sofa, head in hands and

sobbed.

CHAPTER 19

Ti, having finally got over her hysterical sobbing, spoke to her handler who promised to take care of

the situation. We ordered a take- away and talked for hours: Ti was voluble about Andrei and his

legacy of dangerous information. Costas was hearing of it for the first time, as Ti had kept him in the

dark previously, for his own safety. He was incredulous, particularly, I think because she'd been

sharing his flat whilst "on the run", without sharing the fact that he could be endangered by her

presence.

Gramps sent a brief e- mail by his secure server to let us know he'd received all the items and would

be in touch.

At some point in the evening, I remembered to ring Nick and reassure him that I was fine, but that I'd

had to go to Nicosia re the will and would now stay overnight as it was getting late. He was puzzled, but seemed to understand when I said that there was paperwork in which the British Embassy had

to be involved. I told him that I was staying with Costas, whom I'd mentioned to Nick before. That

went down well- Nick was sure I'd be better there than in a hotel alone.

You may wonder why I did not reveal all to Nick just then. As I had picked up my phone to ring him.

Ti caught my eye.

"Nick?" She asked.

I nodded.

"Please don't tell him anything," Ti had asked. "We don't know how we, or rather I, was found, if the

phone theft was more than just a street robbery. There could have been a leak at the lawyer's office,

although the bank is the more likely source. I don't think we were tailed from Paphos to Limassol,

nor from Limassol to here. I made the elementary mistake of repeating my actions- putting the car into the same car park as last time. Perhaps they just waited there in hope that I'd be that stupid.

With luck they'll be picked up and questioned- then we'll know more."

"OK." So I made my uninformative phone call. When I'd finished Ti said,

"Thanks Chloe. When the Putin shit hit the fan, I can emerge from the tomb and Nick can be told

everything."

Provided he hasn't disappeared into the mist, I thought glumly.

Before long Nick rang me back, obviously cross and upset.

"Chloe, what the hell is going on? I've just returned to our flat to find it's been trashed: all the

drawers are open, our suitcases tipped upside down, the bed unmade. Even the stuff in the kitchen

cupboards has been taken out and jars emptied into the sink. Who the hell would do that? Do you

know anything about it?"

"Perhaps it's the same person as last time?" was all I could think of to say.

"Oh no, it's not," Nick responded very quickly.

"How do you know?"

A slight pause, then

"Different ballpark, sweetie. This was a professional job. I'm going to call the police."

"Hold on Nick, just for a moment."

I spoke urgently to Ti.

"Our Flat's been gone over with a toothcomb, should Nick call the police?

She shook her head.

"No, the harm in letting them loose there is that they might miss things or get hurt. Tell him not to

touch anything, to go to an hotel for tonight and we'll sort it from this end."

I realised that she was thinking about the Skripals and the poisoning with nerve agents.

"Nick, Nick my darling, this is important. Don't call the cops. Don't touch anything, not even the

doorknobs. Wash your hands and face- use a tissue to touch the taps. Then leave the flat, check in at

a hotel for the night. Ring me and let me know which one you are in. Please love, do this, it's very

important. I'll be able to explain tomorrow."

"Bloody hell, bloody, bloody hell. Chloe what the fuck is going on?"

Nick sounded devastated, but then rallied,

"OK. I'll get out of here. Speak to you later."

It was nearly midnight when he rang to let me know that he was in Paphos, in one of the big hotels

by the sea. He'd had problems finding anywhere, late September still being the tourist season in

Cyprus. Again he asked me to tell him what I knew, again I reassured him that I would do so in the

morning, but could not say anything now. I told him that I loved him very much.

"Chloe, you are a woman of mystery. A wife of mystery-what more could any man wish? I love you

sweetheart." He blew a kiss, I responded and cut off the call with a quick

"Goodnight love," not wanting to get into telephone sex while sharing a bed with my aunt.

CHAPTER 20.

I found it hard to sleep: too much excitement in the day before meant that again my poor brain would not switch off. Something worried me about my calls with Nick, but I could not identify it.

Ti was sleeping peacefully beside me, her worries now largely over. My feelings about her were complex: I still loved her dearly, but her attitude to Nick had put a wedge between us. Nick- who was now the source of so much of my happiness….my thoughts wandered back to our first meeting in the Jewel Bar.

Ti began to snore gently. It was like old times: when I little and ill or scared at night she was often

the one who'd come to my room, sit on my bed and calm me down. Sometimes she'd lie down

beside me until I went back to sleep. Her comforting smell, that individual odour of a loved one, not

unpleasant, very characteristic with something like roses in it, came back to me now, something I'd forgotten until encountering it again. How fickle our olfactory memories can be: evanescent when

we want to conjure up a smell, but powerfully evocative on actually inhaling it again. It once again lulled me into sleep.

The treble warbling of a mobile phone woke me from a dream in which I was being chased along a

dirt path by a snake. I was sweaty and disorientated. Ti answered her phone, made some mm mm noises of acceptance and said,

"I'll be there in 30 minutes," before switching it off.

"Morning Chlo," she bent down and kissed me on the top of my head, "sleep well?"

"Eventually," I said. "You snore."

"OMG, Andrei was right. I didn't believe him."

"Well, you do. Not loudly, but it does go on and on."

"Sorry love. I've got to go to the Embassy now. Please could you hang on here until I get back?"

"How long will you be?"

"I dunno. Probably a couple of hours. I'll be able to tell you a lot more then- and we can return to

Sea Caves and Nick after that."

I nodded, but asked,

"What should I say to him this morning?"

Ti thought briefly.

"Why not say that there are problems concerning my death certification- but they should be sorted

out soon?"

"O.K."

While we were talking Ti had been dressing hurriedly, now she disappeared from the room. I lay

quietly on my back, eyes closed, allowing myself to fully wake up slowly and comfortably. Suddenly a

thought came unbidden into my mind, the thing that had worried me about Nick's call last night. It

was his rapid and sure denial that the two burglaries in our flat were by the same person, as though he had inside knowledge, perhaps of the first one. My heart literally skipped a beat. Oh Nick!

"Coffee, Chloe?" Costas' voice called from the hall.

"Oh, yes please."

"Can I bring it in to you?"

"Sure," I propped myself up on my pillows, hoping that I did not look too dreadful.

Costas came in, bearing two cups of coffee. He put one onto the table on Ti's side of the bed, then

handed the other to me.

"How are you feeling? Have you recovered from yesterday?
"

"I'm not sure yet. Hope so. How are you?"

"A bit gobsmacked actually. I had no idea what Ti was up to. I can't get over how stupid I was. Did

you know anything?"

"No, nothing."

Ti returned from the bathroom then, so Costas left the bedroom, saying,

"Breakfast in 10 minutes in the kitchen."

"Sorry Costas, I have to go," Ti called after him. "See you both later."

She picked up her cotton jacket from the back of her chair, her handbag from its seat and waved

cheerily to me as she departed.

Ten minutes later, dressed in yesterday's clothes, I joined Costas at the kitchen table. We spent

nearly an hour there, talking things through, catching up on the years we'd been apart. It was very

easy and pleasant until he asked me about Nick. I found myself explaining our first meeting, rapid

romance and then our wedding- but, even to my own ears, it sounded unlikely.

"I look forward to meeting this very lucky chap," said Costas, kindly.

"Oh, I'm the lucky one," I said, blushing.

Ti rang me then, full of enthusiasm.

"Chloe, we did it! Do try and get a copy of the Guardian today- there is an expose of the Putin mega

villa complex, plus documents proving that it does belong to him, at least in part. He passed it off

before as something that his cronies owned. We've nailed that, thanks to Andrei. Should help re-

invigorate the anti- Putin movement."

"That's great, Ti. When are you coming back here?"

"I'm not. At least not yet. We're going through the rest of the material, together with online help

from Gramps. It will take some time to decide how to use it to best advantage. Can you find your

own way home?"

"Probably. Is it safe?"

"Yes, now they know we have the USB and all its contents you should be fine in that little flat. It was checked last night and there's no danger there. Hang on though- you have the keys to the house at

Sea Caves now- why not go there?"

"Which house is it?"

"The white one, set by itself half- way down the road signed Sea Caves, just before you turn into the

road your flat is in. Ring me if you can't find it."

The proposition sounded less and less attractive- but I did not want Ti to think me a wimp so I

agreed to drive back on my own. She'd left my car keys by her side of the bed. Obviously, she'd had

little intention of coming back with me.

"Are you OK Chloe? "Costas looked concerned.

"Yes. Ti is not coming back with me. I have to find the car and drive back on my own."

"No way. After what happened to Ti I am not going to let you do that."

"She says it's safe now- some of the stuff on the USB has been published, so they'll not bother us

anymore."

"Let's not put that to the test. Give me the car keys and the licence plate number. I'll go and find it

and bring it here. Then you can drive it back, but I'll go in front of you in my car to make sure you get

there safely."

"Oh Costas, that would be such a relief. Thank you. "

I gave him a hug.

Whilst Costas was collecting my car, I rang Nick and arranged to pick him up on my way back to Sea

Caves. He said he was enjoying a massive hotel breakfast, trying all the options- so I should look out

for a fat bloke. I laughed, glad that he was in a mood to make jokes.

Costas brought my car to the front door of his block, shepherded me into it, then collected his own to lead me through Nicosia and then to Paphos. The journey passed without incident and we

reached Nick's hotel. Costas wanted to meet Nick so waited in the car park whilst I went to find my

husband. The hotel was very grand, quite intimidating in fact. Nick was nowhere to be seen. I rang

him. There was no answer. I wandered through the lobby and, for a moment, thought I saw Nick's

distant reflection in one of the big mirrors in front of me. Turning round to see if it was him, I lost

sight of the person. It must have been my imagination- or Nick was playing hide and seek. Perhaps

he was sitting in the gardens? They were lush, with groups of palms underplanted with smaller

shrubs, forming little private areas for sitting in the shade- and inimical to an easy search for

someone. After ten minutes and two more unanswered calls it dawned on me to ask at the

Reception desk. I asked for him.

"Mr Nicolaou?" the beautifully dressed girl behind the desk repeated, before checking her

computer.

"Sorry, we do not have anyone with that name staying here. Perhaps he is in one of the other

hotels?"

"Maybe he's checked out?"

The girl fiddled with the keyboard again.

"No, sorry madam, there was no Mr. Nicolaou here last night."

"Thank you."

I made my way to Costas, very worried. There he was in the car park, leaning against his car, reading

a newspaper.

"I can't find him!"

"Perhaps he's gone for a swim?"

"The hotel denies all knowledge of him. Yet I'm sure he said it was this one."

"Have you tried his mobile?"

"Yes, three times."

"Once more for luck then," said Costas reassuringly. "I'm sure he's around here somewhere."

He was right. That time Nick answered. He was coming to the car park to find us. It had all been a big

mistake- he'd given me the wrong hotel name- he'd been so tired looking for somewhere to stay

that he'd got mixed up.

I wanted so much to believe him, even more so when I saw his familiar figure striding across the

asphalt to greet me with a big hug and a kiss.

"Sorry Chloe, I am so stupid. I was in another hotel nearby but got the name wrong."

Then he noticed Costas.

"You must be Costas. Good to meet you," offering his hand. "Thank you so much for looking after my

wife."

Costas took the outstretched hand and shook it.

"A pleasure, as always."

"Should we have lunch all together?" I asked. "My treat."

"It would have been delightful Chloe, but I should get back as I have some work that I need to finish

today. Another time, my dear."

He bent and kissed me gently on the cheek, squeezing my arm as he did so.

"Take great care of her, Nicolaos, she is very special."

"No need to tell me, I know that- and I will."

We waved goodbye as Costas drove off, then Nick said. "He seems like a really nice guy."

"He is, makes a speciality of rescuing me," I replied.

"Well, that's my job now." Nick took my arm and guided me to the car.

"I'll drive and you can tell me what happened on the way home."

I am unsure why but at that moment I decided not to reveal Ti's existence to Nick, at least not yet.

CHAPTER 21

Nick's story

Being back in Cyprus feels good to me. It is my birthplace after all. Michalis, my Dad, was the second

son of his father, Andreas. The family lived in a large stone house with land in a village in the hills

behind Paphos, three generations together. After Michalis married my Mum they also lived with my

grandparents for a while, until after I was born. Then Dad decided to go to England to work with

Uncle Stavros, leaving my Mum and me behind. He knew that his elder brother Demetrios would

inherit the family house and that he needed to find another way to support me and Mum in the long

term. Cyprus did not have much to offer. So Michalis travelled all the way to Larnaca, further than

ever before, then in a plane to England. He was very lost at first, found the language hard, was often cold, hated the grey skies, but he stuck at the job Stavros had found for him. This was as a

waiter in a Greek restaurant, Anemos, in central London. It helped that Michalis had a willing nature,

friendly smile and could dance the Greek dances that the customers loved to see, done ostensibly on

the spur of the moment. The clientele in Anemos were sometimes generous with tips. Michalis stored

these, together with most of his wages, under the ancient mattress in Stavros' rented house. When

he had risen up in the bed by half a centimetre he was able to rent a small restaurant of his own in

North London. Here he decided to keep it simple: just doing a few typical foods, mostly for taking

away. The doner kebab was much in demand: pushed into pitta bread, with salad and drenched with

lemon juice it was a quick, cheap and tasty meal for many local students.

-

Back home Mum and I lived with Yiayia and Grandad,
sharing the house with my uncle Demetrios

and his family: his wife and their daughter Sophia, 2 years
older than me. There was never a time

when Sophia was not important in my life. Apparently soon
after my birth she appointed herself as

my guardian and would sit by me, talking to me and
bringing me toys. She held my hand when I was

learning to walk, then led when I could at last run after her.
We played together all day, every day,

usually in the garden around the house, being spoilt by our
grandparents with home- made sweeties,

like little pieces of shoushouko- a string of almonds inside a
grape juice and flour mixture or karithaki,

a walnut preserved in clove- flavoured syrup. There was
always pitta bread to dip in olive oil and suck

and milk, flavoured with rose syrup, to drink.

Sophia had a doll and that was supposed to be our baby, or
sometimes it was one that we found and

rescued. We were not supposed to go into the fields on our own- there are snakes in Cyprus, mostly

not dangerous, but one, the blunt- nosed viper, can kill humans. The men wore sturdy shoes and long

trousers in the fields, we in our shorts and bare legs would be vulnerable. Sophia liked to push rules

to their limits- and beyond. One day she threw the doll into the field and said to me,

"You have to rescue her. Go on!"

"What about the snakes?"

"Run quickly, they won't catch you then."

"No, I don't want to."

"Scaredy cat, scaredy cat! "

"You threw her, you go."

"No, I'm the mummy. It's the daddy who does rescuing. Go on- or I won't be your friend and I won't

play with you ever again."

That was a terrible threat- worse than that of a snakebite. I ran into the field, grabbed the doll and

turned to come back when something hissed by my leg. Fortunately, I froze. The angry snake twirled

about and slithered rapidly away. I remained there, too scared to move, trembling all over, clutching

the doll to my chest and panting.

"Come on Niko", called Sophia.

"Snake!"

"What?"

"Snake!" It was all I could say.

There was no adult close by to help- Sophia took matters into her own hands, marching into the field

straight up to me, grabbing my hand and leading me back to safety. Once back near the house I burst

into tears.

"What's the matter Nikos?" asked Yiayia.

"Oh, he's just lost a game Yiayia." Sophia was quick witted. "I think a sweet would make him better."

Of course it did, and Sophia got one too. But I never went into the field for years after that.

When I was nearly five years old my dad sent for Mum and me to come to England to live there with

him. It meant that I could grow up learning English at school and have more options in the future, at

least that was how my Dad saw things. He'd sensibly arranged for us to arrive in the summer, so the

weather was good at first and he took us out in the daytime to show us round what he proudly

called" the sights of London." Mum and I were overwhelmed by the size of the place, the grandeur of

some of the buildings, the huge river. My favourite thing was the red double decker buses: riding on

the top deck one could get a good view of the streets below. The number 6 going along Regent, then

Oxford Street was the one I most wanted to catch, partly because it passed the best toyshop in the

world, Hamley's. My parents had promised that we would go into there just before my birthday to

choose my present and I loved to fire up my enthusiasm by repeated near misses. The day we got to

go inside was the best of my life so far. I could not believe the little aeroplanes being flown by the

store assistants, nor the wonderful train set up, the vastness of the Lego supplies. Mum and Dad

were content to let me spend as much time as I liked making my choice of gift, though when I did

there had to be some modification because of financial constraints.

"Can we come back tomorrow? "I said as we left.

"Next year," my Dad replied.

I don't remember missing Sophia very much, my world had become so much more exciting. But she was apparently distraught without me there beside her, obeying most of her whims. School was her

saving grace- she soon made new friends and largely forgot her little cousin. I started school too,

found it miserable at first, never having had to sit still in a chair for long periods of time before. It

wasn't until the third term of my first year that I stopped getting told off for fidgeting or annoying my

neighbours or doing any of the many other things bored children find to amuse them. Then school

began to make sense and I slipped into the routine and started to enjoy myself there. Of course this

was interrupted by the 6 week break for the summer holidays, during which time Mum, Dad and I

went back to Cyprus to see the family.

Even now I can recall the evocative smells, of the sea and of thyme, jasmine, lavender when the plane

doors opened and we were allowed out into the airport when we arrived back. Coming home was so exciting, I could not wait to see Sophia. When we reached the village it was late and dark and she

was asleep, so I had to wait until the next morning.

I was woken from deep slumber by someone using my bed as a trampoline and shouting my name, "

 Nicknik, Nicknik."

Of course, it was Sophia, so happy to have me back. We chattered from then on for most of the next

 several weeks during our waking hours. Goodness knows what we talked about, but I do remember

that it was Sophia who led for Cyprus, making me aware that she was in the better place, London

being a very poor second. I did see a brief flash of green eyes when the red buses and the Hamley's

trip was mentioned, but she merely said,

"OK I'll come with you next time. Let's go and see the chickens and find eggs for breakfast."

After two weeks Dad had to return to London to run the restaurant, Mum and I stayed on for the *whole hot, glorious summer holiday.by the end of it I was berry- brown, scarred from numerous*

scrapes on sea rocks whilst investigating tidal pools, and able to swim.

This pattern was repeated for the next several years, sometimes Sophia would be distant when I

arrived, but would soon succumb and we'd be back on our old friendly brother and sister- type basis

. The need for my Mum to come with me and to stay diminished as I grew older, for a while she too

k me then left after a few days, eventually I did the trip alone. The summer holiday with all three of

us: Dad, Mum and me was never repeated. It did not occur to me to ask why. The answer to my non-

question appeared in the form of Angela, who worked in the restaurant, gradually rose to manage it,

then to manage my Dad's entire life. I don't remember my Mum complaining, at least not in my hearing. She just became quieter and sadder, withdrawing from life outside the two of us. We were close, she and I, more so when Dad stopped coming home to us. Tea was our joint meal, taken soon

after I arrived back from school, usually something cooked and warm, with a cuppa and the radio on.

I can't hear Radio 2 now without thinking of her- and how kind and brave she was, though at the

time I had no knowledge of that- no knowledge, but I hope an instinctive appreciation. She had taken

on a part time job in a local café to supplement what Dad was willing to provide for us but was

always there when I returned from school. I learnt not to ask about Dad and when he'd next come to

see us, as that upset Mum. His visits, weekly at first, became stretched out and finally our connection

with him was only via his Cypriot family- who continued to invite us both year after year. Mum came

with me for the last time when I was sixteen. She was thinner, paler, quieter than I'd known her.

We visited her few, distant relatives in the next village, then settled down at Yiayia's. Grandpa had

died in the winter before and Yiayia was struggling to stay in charge of the house and failing.

Demetrios, her elder son, my Dad's brother, was running things now in the farm, with Eleni his wife

looking after the domestic trivia. Mum and Eleni got on well, so this time Mum stayed for a few

weeks and seemed rested and happier as a result. She'd felt able to take leave from her job at the

café since I was now old enough to leave school and find a job in September on our return. She also, I

later found out, wanted to use the family connections to obtain gainful employment for me.

What did I want? Without thinking I'd assumed that, like my mates, I'd be going back to school after

my GCSEs to do A levels. When Mum mentioned work it came as a deeply unpleasant surprise. I was a callow youth, thinking only of his own needs and desires, not questioning those of others. My world

view changed fast and unalterably when it dawned on me that we were fairly poor, that Mum was

keeping the show on the road and that she was tired of so doing. During the holiday Uncle

Demetrios spoke to me, asked me a few questions about my interests and then, I think, spoke to Dad.

The outcome was a job for me in a small electronic engineering firm in North London, with day

release to study for higher national qualifications. It wasn't my dream job, but then neither was it a

dead end one and I was grateful. That summer I saw very little of Sophia as she had gone on a trip

with a couple of female friends, rail travelling around Europe. She was destined for a secretarial

course on her return. We met for a day or two when she returned- just before Mum and I were due to

leave.

I was quite frankly bowled over by her- somehow she had grown into herself- the gangly legs and

hooked nose now belonged to a still self- assured, but now striking, girl.

"Wow, "I said, "my beautiful cousin!"

We hugged. She was pleased, but a little cool towards me, no doubt having bigger fish to fry.

My mother's death that winter hit me very hard. She had not confided in me about her cancer until

a few months beforehand. I, still callow, had not noticed her declining weight and shortness of

breath until both were very obvious. It seemed to exemplify the injustices in her life: being a kind of

lung cancer, but not related to cigarette smoking- which she'd never done. There was no effective

treatment and in the end she was glad to die to escape the misery of her body. That last Christmas I

treated her like the queen she was: I spent all my wages buying champagne, chocolates, taking her out to Christmas lunch. It was all too late: she was too ill to taste the delicious food, too tired to enjoy

the entertainment and her new dress trailed over her as though on a hanger. My regret about taking

her for granted has not left me yet, I suppose it never will.

Dad came round to the house just before Christmas, looking sad and sheepish, also bearing useless

gifts. Mum agreed to see him, and I took him into the sitting room, where her bed now was located,

and left them together. The adoring look on her face when she saw him sickened me.

After a while he popped his head out and said,

"Your Mum and I would like a cup of tea please, Nikos."

I took in the tray with teapot and two cups, made especially pretty with a cloth, and left him to pour.

They seemed content to be together. Dad looked much happier on departure.

"Come and see us soon, Nikos please," he said. "Angela would like to get to know you."

"I don't want to know her, thank you."

Dad nodded, turned and left. Mum died a few days later in her sleep. I found her, still and grey, in her

bed in the morning and howled and howled. She'd left me a note saying how she loved me and was

so proud of me. I howled some more, before eventually ringing her doctor, not knowing what else to

do.

Our neighbours, Mary and Eddie helped me to organise Mum's funeral. Mary had been Mum's best

friend and was almost as upset as I was. We did her proud. My bouquet- a huge one of white

chrysanthemums, saying MUM, was the best. She'd have loved it, having grown chrysanths in our

little garden to provide colour in the autumn. I chose white ones though, because that's the colour

code for funerals in Cyprus. The funeral director was very respectful, bowing to the coffin, all the others who carried it did too. I know she'd have liked that.

Dad came, without Angela, thank goodness. He was quiet, stood with me in the front row of the

Crem. for the short service. We both wept when the curtains were drawn, and the mechanism started

working, taking her to be burnt. I wanted to leap up and stop it so much.

The next few years were pretty miserable for me. I lived in a hostel near work and saw Dad only very

occasionally. I could not forgive him for what he did to Mum, and I heartily disliked Angela for being

the cause of his defection. However gradually I made friends at the job and at my classes and life

expanded to include football, evenings out, music, girls, and the usual things that young lads do. I also

got into photography, especially that of birds, the feathered kind. It turned out that I was not at all dim: once the usefulness of knowledge became apparent to me, I was able to absorb it and I did well

in my exams and at work. In fact, I had an aptitude for electronic engineering and was promoted

before leaving that firm for another, more progressive one. Having saved a lot from my earnings I

awarded myself a holiday back home in Cyprus. Prompted by Uncle Demetrios I took back to London

an extra case of Cypriot goodies and sold them at a profit to a local restaurant. They wanted more so

Demetrios and I set up a business importing Cyprus foodstuffs: the things that I missed most that

were a lot less tasty in London or were just not obtainable. At first, I sold them myself in a Farmers'

Market in North London, in an area with lots of Greeks and Cypriots. That worked well so we

expanded and now supply many of the London restaurants. COVID hit us hard, so it is fortunate that I kept the day job going- mostly working from home. My other side line is inventing toys and gadgets

for older kids to help their understanding of electronics. That is still making some money as they can

be ordered online, so I am still solvent, just.

CHAPTER 22

It was lovely to be back with Nick again. The animal magic was still working. Sitting next to him in the

little car I could hardly resist touching him, stroking his thigh or the back of his neck where his hair

curled onto his collar. I did stop myself though and concentrated on what to say. I started on the

offensive.

"Do you know a Sophia Nicolaou?"

"Yes, I have a cousin of that name. She lives in Paphos and......Oh, light dawns! Sophia works for a

law firm. Was it the one you went to?"

"Yes. I wondered how she knew we were in a flat in Sea Caves with a nice view."

"She knew because when I let her, and her parents know about our wedding I also told them about

our honeymoon and said we'd see them while we're here. I was going to mention it to you, but kept forgetting, being distracted by the joys of married life. Sorry love."

He steered us round a roundabout then went on.

"Tell me what happened yesterday. It seemed to take forever."

How much to tell? I erred on the side of caution, revealing the happenings in the lawyer's office, but

omitting Ti, Limassol, and the bank, instead moving on to the need to visit Nicosia and the British

Embassy to record the verification of Ti's death and my inheritance.

Out of the corner of my eye I watched Nick closely. He seemed to accept all this nonsense without

demur. We were at Coral Bay by now.

"We should check out the flat first."

Ti had messaged me that it was OK to go there, no signs of neurotoxins or other nasties.

"Sure. Do you have any idea why it was burgled? Or why I was stopped from tidying it up?"

"Not really, but it is OK to go there now. Then we could find the house that I own."

"What?"

"I am the proud owner of a house at Sea Caves, courtesy of Ti's will."

"You're joking!" Nick looked both amazed and pleased.

"No, I have the key in my handbag and the address."

"Is it one of those grand villas by the sea?"

"I don't know. I'll see if I can locate it on Google maps."

I fiddled with my mobile and announced,

"No, it's not one of those, seems to be on the road down to the bend. You know the turn before ours."

"In that case let's go there first."

We did, turning left and descending the steep hill towards the sea. Half- way down was a walled

white house, well- situated in a solitary position with fields around it. There was a security firm notice on the large wooden gate, the number on which was the one on my key ring. Nick turned the

car into the drive and got out to open the gate. A large dog came bounding towards him, barking

threateningly, followed by a man.

"Kalispera" said Nick.

The man responded, "Kalispera" and grabbed the dog's collar.

Nick proceeded to speak to him in Greek, turning and indicating me, obviously explaining that I was

the new owner. The man came up to my window and addressed me.

"Kalispera. You have papers?"

"Yes, I have papers – and a key."

I showed him both. He read the will and the form that the solicitor had given me, then made a phone call. Obviously, that satisfied him and he opened the gates and beckoned Nick to drive into the

grounds.

It is very strange looking round someone else's house in their absence-as many of you who want to

buy a house will do so someday. It feels at the same time fascinating and intrusive, especially when

 the owner is known to you.TV programmes are based on this. The cleaner had been in, so the place

was tidy, but it had an air of waiting for its owner to return, to glance at their reflection in the large

hall mirror, straighten the framed photos, slump on the large sofa, and pick up the book left on the

table beside it. If I had not already known that Ti was alive, I might have inferred it from the feeling

in this house. I could hardly walk around it. Nick had no such inhibitions. He went careering

from room-to-room downstairs, then did the same upstairs, keeping up a running commentary on the house.

"Nice study, good sitting room, elegant staircase. Wow, great big balcony here. Super views too,

nearly as good as the flat."

Eventually he returned to me, still standing in the hall studying the photo of Ti and Andrei on what I

guessed was their wedding day. Andrei looked genuinely happy; Ti was radiant. It looked like a real

love match. I hoped it had been.

"Oh, my darling, I am so thoughtless."

Nick took me into his arms and held me close. I breathed in the smell of him, compounded of after

shave, male sweat, and the individual odour that was uniquely his.

"Let him be a goody, please let him be a goody," I thought, enjoying the moment of peace.

"Better now," I said. "How about giving me a guided tour?"

Nick enjoyed taking me round to see what he'd discovered. The bed in the master bedroom was freshly made up.

"Should we move in today?" Nick asked.

"Why not? Let's check out of the flat, pay for a tidy up there and bring our stuff over."

That is what we did. Afterwards we walked down the hill to the coast road and had a sundowner at

Sea Caves Gardens, followed by supper at Nature, the restaurant opposite. Too late I remembered

about buying a paper copy of the Guardian, but I found the article on my phone.

"What's that you're studying so intently?"

"Stuff about Putin and his palace by the sea. I like to check out others like us, with seaside palaces."

Nick laughed and looked at the article on my phone. Then he said,

"We're losers though love, ours doesn't have an underground skating rink, nor 2 helicopter pads."

"Give us time."

We walked home arm in arm, accompanied by moonlight, stars and the sounds of the sea.

CHAPTER 23.

The new bedroom was much larger and the bed more comfortable than in the flat. We both slept

late, then had tea on the balcony in our pyjamas.

"You know I promised Sophia that we'd see her?"

I nodded.

"Well how about we give a party here, a late wedding celebration? There's plenty of room. We could

invite Sophia and her Mum and Dad, there are a few other rellies, Costas could come too."

Nick was very enthusiastic. I realized that he wanted to show them our new house, to affirm that he

had made it bigtime. I was happy to oblige.

"Of course, provided I don't have to cook."

"No problem. We can ask Nature to cater for us, they are not very busy at this time of year. In any

case you can bet your bottom dollar that all my rellies will bring things to eat. They always do."

"When should we have it, at the weekend?"

"Good idea- on the Sunday, I think. Everyone will be already booked up for Saturday."

So, it was settled. Nick set to calling his various Cyprus relatives, I rang Costas who was keen to come.

"What about Ti?" he asked. Nick was out of earshot.

"I'd like to, but it might be a bit insensitive since it'll be in the last place that she lived with her

husband before he died."

"Would you like me to speak to her about it? She's staying in Lefkosia for the time being."

"Yes, please do- and let me know what she says. Thanks Costas."

If she decides to come then I am going to have to explain to Nick that Ti is still alive, I thought, and

just why I have been lying to him. Oh dear.

Planning the party was great fun. It was the first time we had done anything like that together: our wedding having been taken over by my very efficient mother from the start. Think Mrs Thatcher

minus several years of age and you'll get an idea of her. We decided to go for a cosmopolitan buffet

feast and chatted to the chef at Nature about what it should contain. I made sure to tell him to avoid

pistachios and cashew nuts absolutely. Nick thought we should drink Cyprus wine- that gave us a

good excuse to go round the various vineyards sampling them. In the end we decided on a white

wine, Vassilikon, from the Kathikas winery up the hill from Sea Caves and a red, Status 99, from

Kolios winery. The beer was also Cypriot: Nick bought both Keo and Leon as he knew the tastes of his

various relatives differed. He also indulged in an orange liqueur, Filfar. This claimed to be" a subtle

blend of sun-ripened oranges with aromatic herbs from the hillsides, handed down since the

Venetian era. Tangy but mellow warmly golden, distinctively Cypriot." It was delicious (we had a

secret tasting from the bottle after supper on the night before the party).

Decorating the house and garden was also time-consuming, but fun. Nick drove us to the mall,

where he'd recently spent many hours waiting for me, as he did not hesitate to remind me. There

we entered Jumbo, which gave us what I call the IKEA experience, that is once you get in you must

go all the way round in order to leave. One down from the Hotel California experience. The shop was jam -packed with stuff- I felt giddy from looking around so much whilst smelling lots of plastic.

However, it did have lots of cheap, tacky, but useful solar lights for the garden, candles for the house,

metal balloons, streamers etc. We ended up with a full trolley, not so cheap after all in terms of

money and the environment.

We'd contacted Sophia, who was delighted with the invitation, and her parents, who also agreed to

come. They put Nick in touch with various other relatives of his, most of whom accepted our

invitation. That made some twenty in all. In a burst of enthusiasm we invited our Airbnb host, who

lived in Paphos and Mr Antoniades, the lawyer, who pleaded an alternative engagement. The

cleaner, who'd been retained, came on the party morning to make the house shine- and was

promptly invited, along with our guard too, plus his dog. It was going to be quite an event.

Suddenly I had a thought.

"What about music? Surely we should have some?"

Nick had the answer. There was a small speaker in the house- into which he could attach his mobile

and play his Spotify playlist. Unfortunately, he had no control over the order of the music played, as his account was a freebie- but we'd have to put up with that.

We spent the morning in a flurry of anticipation, hardly managing to concentrate on anything not

party- related. I did manage to read online another Guardian article derived from the USB content,

having been alerted by a text from Beatrice Epstein. This one detailed the involvement of Putin in

the murder of one of his associates, not Boris Berezovsky. The USB had obviously held many secrets

and these were being revealed piecemeal to maximise their impact upon forthcoming elections.

Finally, the sun began its slow descent towards the sea, the air cooled and the solar lights we'd

placed along the driveway came on.

"Hey, time to change!"

For Nick it was easy, just a smart shirt and clean trousers. For me there was not much choice- I had brought only two dresses, so I wore the red one that I had not worn to the lawyer's office, with my

one pair of heels. I brushed my hair, pinned it back at one side with a grip into which I placed

a red rose from the still flowering bush in the garden. We were ready.

Sophia arrived first, driving a nippy- looking, low slung blue sports car. She emerged from it without

difficulty, impressing me considerably, and came straight up to me, taking my hand and giving me a peck on each cheek.

"Chloe, how good to see you again- and not in the office this time. I didn't realise that NickNick

hadn't told you that I'd be there. Never mind- we can get to know each other now. I love that rose in

your hair- so pretty."

My heart sank. Nick had said that he didn't mention it because he didn't know which lawyer she worked for. A small untruth, but I hate being lied to. The way she called my husband Nick Nick

reminded me of knickknack and seemed too intimate. I found it offensive. However, I rallied and

thanked her.

"Come and get a drink, then I'll show you the house, if you like." said Nick.

"Oh, hi NickNick." She pecked his cheek. "I like. Thank you."

Nick shepherded her into the kitchen where we'd laid out drinks and glasses. I watched them, easy

together, his arm loosely behind her at waist level, faces almost touching, smiling and was green-

eyed. Sophia was dark- haired, dark eyed, lithe, with a nose too prominent and hooked for true beauty, but she was certainly striking. What did Nick see in me?

Various Nicolaou relatives appeared at intervals. Nick's Aunt Eleni and Uncle Demetrios were delightful, very warm, and pleasant to me. They told me stories of Nick as a little boy and how he was sometimes led astray by their daughter. I liked to hear about what he was like and wanted to

respond with stories about Ti, our family's wild child, but thought it best to leave her name out of the evening. Everyone wanted to see round the house, all were very complimentary. Eleni was sweet, she said to me,

"I think you would rather have your aunt alive than have this house, wouldn't you?"

I nodded,

"Of course, I would. Family is so important," thinking what a hypocrite I was with Ti alive and kicking somewhere in Nicosia. I hoped to Heaven that she did not turn up. You could never tell with Ti.

When most of our guests had arrived, we encouraged them to eat the delicious food which had been beautifully displayed on our dining table. It was hard at first to get anyone to ruin the display and start eating, but I persuaded Eleni to break the ice and fill a plate, then Demetrios followed and soon everyone began queueing. People are funny, aren't they?

When most of the people had eaten the first course Nick turned up the music and led me out onto the balcony to dance. I have a good sense of rhythm, can move well to music and love dancing. We were soon joined by Sophia with one of her second cousins, then Eleni and Demetrios came out too and began to dance in a more old- fashioned, conjoined way. By now it was darker, cooler too, but not cold. The stars were appearing as the sky blackened, the sea could be heard whenever the music paused. It was wonderful.

Then I remembered the desserts.

"We haven't had pudding!" I turned to go in, Nick followed, and we cleared the table together, putting uneaten food into containers in the fridge and dumping the Jumbo paper plates in the recycling. We were a good team. Nick found the desserts- which he'd decided upon and stored in the fridge. As we were transferring them to the table Sophia entered the kitchen.

"Oh, I nearly forgot. I brought something too. It's in the car."

She returned with a large circular container and opened it to reveal a cake. It was covered by swirled pink and white icing and had pomegranate seeds packed tightly all round it sides. From it came a delicate smell of roses

"It's a Persian Love Cake. I made it specially for you."

From her handbag she retrieved a small package. This turned out to be a decoration for the top of the cake, a little bridal couple.

"Oh Sophia, that is lovely. How very kind of you. Thank you so much." I kissed her on the cheek, beginning to warm to her.

"That deserves a place of honour in the centre of the table."

I placed it there and found more smaller paper plates and napkins, also white and silver. Again the table looked pretty and inviting. I began asking our guests to come and sample the desserts.

"Let's leave the cake until last," said Nick "then we can be photographed cutting it, like in our real wedding."

"Sure- and those who are already FTB can take some home with them."

"FTB?"

"Full to bursting."

As often happens at childrens' birthday parties most guests were too full to eat cake - so at the end

 of the evening we were busy wrapping up slices in napkins for home consumption. Those who did

try it were very complimentary, with some praising it as the best cake ever. Gradually the house

emptied, with Nick's rellies seeming satisfied with our celebration, giving us lots of thanks and nice

remarks.

Eleni told me,

"I am so glad Nick has found you. He needed someone to love and care for- and you are perfect for

him."

I was a little worried that she was referring to my disability but said nothing other than that Nick was

perfect for me too.

Eventually the only remaining guest was Sophia who kindly offered to help with the washing up.

"There's not a lot, thanks. We deliberately used paper plates to reduce the load."

"Let me do the glasses then."

There were loads of them. Most people must have used more than one each. I went round the

house and garden, finding them all, or nearly all.

When the clearing up was finished Sophia asked me.

"Did you try my cake?"

I had to be honest,

"Sorry no, I simply could not manage to eat any more."

"Oh please just have a mouthful, one mouthful. I want to know what you think of it. The recipe is

from Ottolenghi and I think you will like it a lot."

She cut me a smallish slice, put it onto a clean plate and handed it to me.

"It goes well with white wine." Sophia poured me a glass of that too.

I was tired, a little drunk and the last thing that I wanted or needed was more food or more wine,

but Sophia had obviously made a big effort and I did want to disappoint her.

"Thank you, Sophia, you are very kind." I took a mouthful of the surprisingly dense cake and the

mingled tastes of pomegranate, rose, lemon and almond filled my mouth.

"Oh it is wonderful!"

"Nick, have you tried it?"

He had not but consented to have a bite from my slice.

"Very good."

"I am so glad you like it. Now I really must go, I have to get up early tomorrow. Goodbye Nick."

Sophia brushed his cheek with her lips, then bent to kiss me too.

"Bye Chloe."

Nick walked with her to her car. I could just hear him trying to persuade her to stay overnight, but

she was adamant about leaving. I felt glad when I heard the powerful engine start and the

headlights moved across my field of vision as she reversed out of our gate. I had Nick all to myself.

Suddenly I felt ill: nauseous with sharp pains in my stomach. I hurried to the loo and arrived just in

time to throw up in it. I felt faint and stayed on the ground by the loo, head bent low.

Nick returned inside to find me like this.

"Chloe, what's the matter? Are you drunk?"

"No. Please ..my handbag..quickly."

I had recognised what was happening, the itching all over sensation had arrived together with

difficulty in breathing. This was anaphylaxis, rearing its ugly head again after so many years of absence. What I needed was my adrenalin pen- which was in my handbag upstairs. I could hear Nick

moving around nearby.

It took all the effort I could muster to whisper

"Bedroom."

He was climbing the stairs, but slowly, far, far too slowly.

I was sick again, this time on the floor and on myself. I felt too ill to care and did what I'd been

taught: to lie down with my legs propped up- on this occasion on the handy loo. Breathing was

becoming harder, so I tried to prop myself up a little.

Nick returned with my handbag.

" Ad.." was all I could say.

He nodded and searched through the bag.

"It's not here, bloody hell, where is it?"

He tipped all the contents onto the vomit- covered floor. There was a blue inhaler, but no adrenalin auto injector.

"Blue…."

Nick picked up the blue inhaler and puffed it into my open mouth twice.

"More"

He obliged, giving me several puffs.

"Suitcase."

I always kept a spare adrenalin pen in my suitcase- which was also in my bedroom. Nick hurried off

again. There was another wave of nausea, the terror of approaching death hit me and then the

world went dark.

CHAPTER 24

Costas' story

It had been a difficult journey from Nicosia. If I'm honest that was partly my fault because I'd started

late, having got involved in a project and worked on it for too long. That's one of the problems with

working from home- the lack of definition of start and end times. I am not good at routine. Also, I'd

rather hoped that Ti would change her mind and come with me. I know just how much she means to

Chloe. However, Ti was adamant that she needed to lie low for a while longer- until the facts about

Putin's misdeeds had all been drip- fed to the world, with a final roll call emerging just before the

next elections in Russia. She feared that if known to be alive she could be captured and used as a

hostage to prevent full disclosure.

I'd also forgotten to prime the sat nav or use Google maps on my phone. Sea Caves is not hard to find, but once there the roads are a nightmare, leading you on and then suddenly ending in a cul de sac or a steep dip via a muddy track to reach the sea. It was ages since I'd been there, and I had no memory of the geography. Still, I set off along the motorway towards Paphos thinking that I'd arrive for the later part of the party, often the best bit with old friends hanging around to chat. The blow out took me by surprise- it happened on the beautiful stretch of road along by Petrou tou Romiou, the place where Aphrodite came ashore. There was a bang then my car swung wildly towards oncoming vehicles. I used all my strength to bring it back onto my carriageway and ease it onto the miniscule hard shoulder. It was getting dark and changing the tyre was a frightening and frustrating experience. Fortunately, it was not on the driver's side, otherwise I'd not have been able to do it. The nuts had been tightened by the garage using a machine, getting them off was tough, even after liberal application of the WD 40 that luckily, I had with me. While I struggled, I was dimly aware of the lights and siren of a police car passing on the opposite side of the road, ten minutes later it returned, this time on my side and stopped just behind me, lights still flashing.

"Need any help sir?" the policeman asked in Greek.

I accepted gladly and together we got the spare tyre on and the holed one, which had a nail

protruding from it, went into the boot.

"You're the second one today", said the cop. " Someone must have dropped nails on the road,

probably fallen out of an old door or something."

I swore.

"Yes, I second that. Never mind, you're good to go now."

"Efharisto."

I drove off, careful not to exceed the speed limit. Without the sat nav I could not find the shorter

back route and had to go right into Paphos and out again to reach Sea Caves. Sunday night was in

full swing, lockdown a thing of the past so the roads were crowded with revellers. Not only that,

every other one was crawling along looking for somewhere to park. Finally, I found myself beyond the fleshpots of Coral Bay only 5km from my destination. That 5km took me over half an hour- I had been round various bits of Sea Caves several times before I saw the house, as Ti had described it, standing slightly alone above the sea. It was brightly lit and had a festive air, so I thought it still worth seeing if the party was ongoing. For some reason I had a feeling that I needed to arrive, though by now I had lost any vestige of party spirit.

The drive was empty, apart from the small car that I remembered Chloe driving. I parked mine and

hurried to the door. I knocked loudly as there was music playing inside. Nothing happened. I knocked again, even louder. My breath was coming in short gasps-God knows why.

Suddenly the door opened and there was Nick, silhouetted against the light from inside. He looked

dreadful: pale, sweaty, haunted, tears running down his face.

"What's the matt…" I saw beyond him through the open into the downstairs cloakroom Chloe lying motionless. I ran to her.

"Chloe, Chloe.." there was no response, but she had a faint thready pulse and I thought I detected

breathing. She was covered in what looked like a nettle rash. I knew what was wrong. We'd been

through this before when she was little. Katherine, her mother, had taught everyone who looked

after Chloe what to do in the event of her having the severe allergic reaction called anaphylaxis.

"Has she had adrenalin?"

Nick shook his head.

"It's not in her handbag."

I saw that he was standing by a suitcase.

"In there?"

Nick did not answer. He looked dazed.

I opened the suitcase. It was empty. I felt inside the outer pockets and my grateful fingers

encountered a cylindrical object. Thank God- it was an adrenalin pen. It even had small pictures on it demonstrating how it should be used. As directed, I removed the blue top, cursing as my nervous

fingers fumbled with it. Then I plunged the other end into Chloe's unresisting thigh, felt the click as

the mechanism released the adrenalin into her muscles, waited for 10 seconds then withdrew the pen

and massaged the area hard. Then I began compressing her chest rhythmically to get blood flowing

to distribute the life -saving adrenalin. For a long minute nothing happened, then she shuddered,

opened her eyes and blinked. I stopped the chest massage, somewhat embarrassed.

"Chloe, how are you?"

"Awful, I feel sick..." She turned her head away from me and vomited. I nearly did so too.

"My head is throbbing. Water please"

I glanced up at Nick. He was still standing there, looking lost.

"Water please, Nick," I said. He visibly pulled himself together and went to get some.

"Did you find my pen? The adrenalin?"

I nodded.

"Thank you, Costas, you've rescued me again." She smiled weakly.

Nick handed her a glass of water and she sipped from it.

"What the hell was in that cake?" Chloe asked.

"What cake?" I asked

"The one Sophia made for us, Persian Love Cake."

"They are made with almond flour, I think. That shouldn't bother you. It's only cashews and

pistachios you're allergic to, isn't it, or has that changed?"

"Not as far as I know- but I haven't been tested for years."

"Well we need to take you to the hospital now."

"Oh no, I'm fine, really I just want to stay here quietly."

"Chloe, you know what your Mum taught us all- if you use your adrenalin pen you must go to the

hospital in case there is a second wave of the reaction."

I think I got COVID and anaphylaxis mixed up in talking about waves, what I'd meant was a late reaction.

Nick intervened.

"She's fine now, let her stay here."

"Sorry, no way. Come on Chloe." I helped her up from the floor, wiped her down with a wet flannel

and then simply picked her up and carried her to my car.

"Bring her handbag please Nick – and some money. Chloe will need another adrenalin pen.

CHAPTER 25

I felt terrible again: heart pounding, sweaty, sick, and faint. The adrenalin had revived me for about

 half an hour, but I could feel myself sliding back into anaphylaxis. Fortunately, Costas had made me lie down on the back seat of the car. He and Nick were in front, Costas driving, Nick navigating us to the nearest hospital using his phone. I must have passed out again because the next thing I knew I was lying on something very uncomfortable (it turned out to be a trolley), with an oxygen mask on my face and rapid beeping in the background, all under harsh lighting. My arm was being held immobile whilst someone inept was trying to get a needle into my veins. Fortunately, that person was relieved by another, more ept, individual who managed to take blood and put up a drip fast and largely painlessly. As the saline flowed into me, I began to improve: I could breathe and think more easily.

"Thank you," I said to all those around me, meaning the drip fixer.

"How are you doing Chloe?" he asked.

"Much better, thanks. Did you give me more adrenalin?"

"Sure did. And a few other things too. Do you feel up to answering a few questions?"

I nodded. We went over my long history of allergies and of anaphylaxis- to egg and milk when I was

little, later outgrown, then to nuts- for some unknown reason just cashews and pistachios.

"What do you think caused tonight's reaction?" the doctor asked.

"It happened soon after I started eating a special cake, a Persian love cake. I don't know what's in it,

but I think it had almond flour. That's not usually a problem for me though."

"Katerina, can you come in here a minute?"

The person who'd been fiddling with my arm reappeared between the curtains of my cubicle. She

looked sad and dark- eyed with tiredness.

"Yes. What do you want?"

"What's in a Persian love cake?"

"Oh it varies, usually butter, eggs, almond flour, rosewater, lemon, pistachios, sometimes ginger…."

"Pistachios!" The male doctor and I said it together.

"Jinx"

"Well, no more Persian love cake for you Chloe", he said. "Always ask about contents in future, remember? Your husband said you vomited a few times, is that right?"

 I nodded.

"Well then, there's probably not much cake left in your stomach to be absorbed and cause further

problems. I propose we keep you here until morning and then if you are OK you can go home with

two fresh adrenalin pens and I'll resupply your asthma inhalers. You've had intravenous

corticosteroid just now to prevent any late response and to help open up your breathing tubes, but

you must use your preventer inhaler every day without fail."

"I do, I really do, "I assured him. He continued writing in my notes.

"Good girl." Turning to Katerina he said

"Keep her monitored here overnight. Write her up for the meds will you- and check on her at

7.30am. if she is stable, she's good to go."

He finished his notes, signed them with a flourish, bade me goodbye and disappeared through the

curtains. Katerina sighed and began to write on another chart.

"Please could I see my husband?" I ventured.

"In a minute. What's his name?"

"Nicolas Nicolaou."

She said nothing more but disappeared out of the curtains and soon Nick appeared through them.

He hesitated for a second before coming to my side, the one minus the drip, and taking my hand

bent to kiss me, giving out a sigh of relief as he did so.

"Chloe, my darling! Are you OK? I was so worried."

"I'm fine now. Just got to stay here till morning though."

"Poor you. It doesn't look very comfortable."

"No, I've known better beds. Never mind I'll be home soon."

"That's good. I'll come back to get you."

I was surprised that he was not thinking of staying with me all night himself and must have shown

that in my expression, because he went on

"I have something important to do."

"Oh, I see." When this had happened to me as a child my parents had always seen to it that one of them was with me or close by at all times. Perhaps it was wrong for me, as an adult, to expect that, even after a near- death experience.

"Has Costas gone home?"

"No, he's still here. Do you want to say goodnight to him?"

"Please."

Nick kissed me again, then left and Costas entered the cubicle a few minutes later. He stood by the

curtain looking intently at me. There were tears in his eyes.

"Thank God Chloe. Thank God you survived. Thank God your mother taught us all what to do when it

happens. Thank God." He was shaking his large head slowly from side to side as he said this and

slowly moving towards me. He put his hand on my forehead as a kind of blessing as he said the last

thank God.

"Costas, please tell me what actually happened. I only remember feeling sick and ill in the bathroom

and Nick searching for my handbag to get my adrenalin pen- but it wasn't there."

"When I arrived, you were unconscious on the bathroom floor, Nick was totally lost. He seemed

dazed. I spotted your suitcase, found the pen in it and gave it to you according to the instructions.

You came round and we got you into the car. I remembered to keep you lying flat- but you went

unconscious again when we were nearly here. I carried you in, shouting the Greek word your Mum taught us,

"Anaphylaxis. Anaphylaxis. She needs adrenalin fast please."

"I said it all in Greek- the Receptionist motioned to me to carry you straight in and a nurse helped me put you onto the nearest couch. The sister of the A and E department rushed up, syringe in hand and gave you something, no questions, quick as a wink. Then they wheeled you into a cubicle and got the doctors in to see you. The rest you know."

"Oh Costas, you saved me yet again, thank you. One day I'll have to save you."

I took his hand and kissed it.

"How do you feel now?"

"A bit washed out, but the pain in my guts and the nausea have gone. I think I vomited up most of the cake. They think I'll be able to go home in the morning."

"You are amazing Chloe. The last time I saw you do this you bounced back so quickly I could hardly

believe it. Near death to active life, remarkable."

"I'm not so young anymore, the bounce back may take longer."

"Hmmm. You still seem young to me, even though you are now a married woman."

"And beautiful too no doubt?"

"Of course."

"You are a wonderful flatterer Costas." I kissed the hand, which I was still holding, again.

"You should try to get some sleep; Nick and I will wait outside."

"Nick is thinking of not staying," I paused, "probably going home to get the place cleared up. Then he'll come back for me."

"Oh." That oh spoke volumes. "Then I'll stay here in case you need me. Rest now Chloe, you are safe."

He bent and kissed my forehead, then left. I half expected Nick to return and say goodbye, but he did not. I closed my eyes and attempted to drift off to sleep- not easy when full of adrenaline, the fight or flight hormone. Do you know that state somewhere between wakefulness and sleep? The brain is in free fall, thoughts are jumbled, but sometimes crystallize due to unexpected associations.

Lying on that couch I linked the absence of the adrenalin pen from my handbag to the burglary at our Sea Caves Airbnb. I could not remember seeing the pen when I picked up the handbag contents- but had not realised its loss at the time. The handbag had been under the bed, perhaps the pen had fallen out and was there? I resolved to go and find out. Having resolved that I fell asleep, only to be woken by the nurse doing my observations half an hour later.

CHAPTER 26

Next morning Nick arrived, looking almost as tired as I felt. Costas had fared better- he'd been found a couch to lie on by one of the nurses who'd taken a shine to him and had slept quite well. We exchanged greetings then, once I was given my medicines and discharged, left the building together.

"You'd better come home with us Costas", said Nick.

"Sure, my car is still at your house. I'd like to see the house too, if that's OK?"

"Of course. Have breakfast with us as well."

I was glad that Nick was being welcoming to Costas. Both men were hugely important in my life.

Walking between the two of them to the car I felt like a queen.

On the drive home up the coast I asked,

"Please could we go to the Sea Caves flat?"

"Why?" Nick asked.

"I want to look for my adrenalin pen under the bed. I think it fell out of my handbag when the intruder dropped it."

"Intruder?"

Costas knew nothing of the incident, so I told him the brief details on the way there.

"Very odd", he said.

Fortunately, we'd returned the keys to the key safe on the wall and were able to retrieve them using the same code as before. We all went into the block, a dog barked downstairs on hearing the key in the outer door and again when I turned the key in the door of the flat. That gave me an idea.

First I checked under our double bed: no adrenalin pen, but some dust- so it had not been cleaned away.

Nick was showing Costas the amazing views from the balcony.

"Any luck?"

"No, it's not there."

"Maybe the cleaner found it."

"It hasn't been cleaned yet- we left early."

"Umm."

On the way out the dog barked again. I excused myself from the two men, saying I'd meet them at

 the car, descended the stairs to the door of the dog flat and knocked on it. Ferocious barking

ensued, then an angry female voice,

"Shut up."

The door was opened by an elderly lady with grey hair and beautiful facial bone structure.

"I'm really sorry to bother you. We were living upstairs in the flat and we had a burglary. I wondered

if you'd heard or seen anything?"

"Oh dear, that's awful. I am so sorry. Did you lose much?"

"Fortunately no, but it would be good to catch the burglars. I thought your dog might have barked."

"Oh, Holly barks at anything and everything. But now you mention it she went crazy a few nights ago-in the night. I heard the front door slam and a car drove away. I looked out of my front window, but I was too late to see anyone."

She paused.

"I did see a young girl though, not like you. I mean she was not you."

"When was that?"

"Hard to say, every day is much the same. It was before the night- time incident, and it was in the day, just before Holly's afternoon walk. "

"What was the girl like?"

"Tall, dark, with long hair. She left in a little blue car."

"Thank you so much. You've been very helpful."

I returned to the car.

"Any luck?" asked Nick.

"No, none at all."

CHAPTER 27

Costas returned to our new house with us in order to see it and to collect his car. He was very impressed by its situation on a small knoll, giving good views all around and by the light spacious rooms.

"Just like Felicity to find somewhere nice."

I nodded, frowning briefly at him, out of view of Nick, as a warning not to talk about Ti. Nick still did not know she was alive.

"What would you like for breakfast Costas? We have bread, cereals, eggs, cheese et cetera."

"Bread please with cheese and some olives if you have them."

I have never understood the liking of Europeans for that sort of food at breakfast- but was happy to oblige. Nick voted for scrambled eggs and toast. I joined him in that choice.

We sat round the circular dining table, eating, drinking coffee and enjoying the sunlight pouring in.

Nick was asking Costas about the projects he was working on. I was quiet, trying to piece together my thoughts. The burglar could have been a girl who drives a sports car. Was that Sophia? If so what

was she doing? Was it removing my adrenalin pen from my handbag? Did she know about my allergies? Was the cake with pistachios a deliberate attempt to harm me? To kill me? If so, why?

Presumably the motive would have been money. Apparently, I was now seriously rich. Though I had

no idea yet of the value of the investments and bitcoin which Ti had bequeathed me, the house we were in must be worth a couple of million euros at least. Finally, what was I going to do now? Staying in the house with Nick did not seem sensible since if Sophia was the burglar he might be involved. I remembered that he'd thought the second burglary was different from the first- for no immediately

obvious reason. I had an idea.

"Costas, please could I have a lift with you when you leave?"

"Yes, of course. To Lefkosia?"

I could tell he thought that I wanted to see Ti.

"Yes, I'd forgotten that I have to return to sign more forms today. Just remembered."

"I can take you love, then there'll be no problems about getting back," Nick interjected.

"No thanks, Nick. It is going to be boring stuff. I'll go with Costas. If it's late I'll stay overnight and come back tomorrow. You have a fun day here. You can snorkel to your heart's content."

"I can bring you to Limassol tomorrow as I've got to go there. You can get a bus back to Paphos from there," Costas offered

"That would be good."

"OK, as you wish." Nick was obviously miffed. "It's only our honeymoon."

"Sorry love, I promise to spend all my time with you when I get back. I'll get my stuff."

I hurried upstairs and packed my suitcase with all my medicines, nightwear, and a change of clothes.

Nick gave me a big hug and a loving kiss when I came down again.

"I'll miss you, my darling."

"Me too."

We kissed again and I left with Costas.

As we drove away Costas asked me "What's going on Chloe?"

"Oh God, I wish I knew. The lady in the flat downstairs said she seen a girl who wasn't me leave the block and drive off in a sports car. That could have been Sophia. She might have removed the adrenalin pen from my handbag, then given me cake with pistachios in to eat."

"My God Chloe, that is some accusation."

"I know, but she is the secretary to the lawyer who read Ti's will to me. She knows that I am very wealthy."

"How would she know about your allergies?"

"Sophia is Nick's cousin."

"Bloody hell!"

"Precisely. That's why I did not want to be left alone with Nick. If it was Sophia, then he might be involved. I just don't know what to think. I love Nick. I think he loves me, but I just don't know any more."

Tears came to my eyes, I brushed them away.

"What should I do Costas? I can't run away forever. Perhaps I can just give all the money away?"

"Let's stop somewhere, I want to look up something on my computer."

We turned off the main road and parked outside the Lucky Genie.

"More coffee?" asked Costas.

"Sure."

I followed Costas inside and he led to me to the table furthest from the counter. We ordered coffees

and waited until the waiter had gone.

Costas was already checking his laptop.

"It says here that if you were to die without making a will everything you own would pass to your husband."

"That's what I thought."

"Well, there's your answer: make a will excluding Nick. Do it today, sign it and you'll be safe."

"Except for the Russians!"

"I think your quick action with that USB has seen them off. I really hope so."

"Do you think the two are linked?"

"Maybe, does Nick have any past history of political activity?"

"No idea, but if he were a spy surely his past would be clean as a whistle?"

"Probably."

I was silent for a while, sipping my Cyprus coffee thoughtfully.

"The will is a good idea Costas. Easier and quicker than resurrecting Ti. Should I do it through the

lawyer who employs Sophia, so she knows about it?"

"Yes. Let's write it now, email it to that lawyer, asking for it to be signed and witnessed later today.

There'll be templates for wills somewhere on the internet."

He tapped away and then, "Got one- copying it, pasting it. Now look at it."

The only will I'd seen thus far in my life was Ti's. This looked similar. I filled in my personal details

and made disbursements of my wealth, all of it to charities, even the Sea Caves house.

"Will this do?"

Costas checked what I'd done.

"Looks fine. Please send it by e- mail to the lawyer and copy it to someone safe and independent."

I did that, including in the email that I would be coming into the office to sign it today, together with a witness.

"Please would you come with me and witness the will?"

"Sure Chloe. For you, anything."

"Let's go then."

Sophia was not there. We were greeted by an older lady whom I had not met before.

"How can I help you?" she asked.

"Oh, I am just here to sign my will. I e- mailed it to Mr Antoniades this morning. If you could please

print it out for me I'll sign it in front of him.

"Oh, that's not the way we do these things. You need to speak to him first, then the will gets written,

then you come back with an appointment to sign it."

"No, that is not the way I do these things. Time is important. Either it is printed now, and we sign it in

front of Mr Antoniades, or I take it elsewhere. I think Mr Antoniades will agree to help."

"Let me just have a quick word with him. Please sit down in the waiting room."

She knocked on the lawyer's door, then entered, shutting it behind her. A few minutes later she emerged and called us into the office.

Mr A was as smarmy as ever.

"Chloe, my dear, how lovely to see you. How are you enjoying your new home?"

"Very much, thank you. You suggested I should make a will. I have and I wish to sign it now. Costas

can be a witness."

"Mrs Georgiou, please print three copies now."

While she was occupied Mr A read through what we had written on his computer. He glanced up at me.

"Nothing for your family? Are you sure?"

"Absolutely."

Mrs Georgiou returned with the documents, and we signed them Costas and I, with Mrs Georgiou as

the other witness. Mr A was designated as my executor.

I was given a copy to keep. This I tucked into my handbag, alongside the new adrenalin pen. I was safe. I thanked Mr A and asked after Sophia.

"Most unusually she has not turned up for work today and is not answering her phone. Sophia is usually so reliable.

Mrs Georgiou does part time work for me and this is fortunately one of her days in the office."

"Oh, I am sorry. I hope she is not ill."

"Me too. I hope she has not gone down with COVID."

Costas and I returned to his car.

"What now Chloe?" he asked.

Precisely. What now? Did I return to Nick, still unsure of whether he'd played a part in my near death experience? Should I go with Costas to Nicosia and talk to Ti? I decided on the latter.

"Please can I come home with you? I'd like to see Ti."

"No problem. In you get."

The road from Paphos to Nicosia (called Lefkosia by Costas) was gaining in familiarity so I sat back and relaxed, as the pilot suggests on an aeroplane, trying to decide what to do about my future. I loved Nick as the man I thought he was, no doubt about that; was he really that person or was he a scheming bastard who'd married me knowing I would soon be rich? And one who'd connived in trying to bump me off? I went over and over the memories of times with him, my heart fighting with my head.

CHAPTER 28

Nick's story

I left Chloe in the hospital with a nasty mixture of anxiety and murder in my heart. Sophia had known about Chloe's allergy to pistachios, I was pretty sure of that. I thought that it was one of the many things I had told her during our What's App calls. I tried to go over them in my head as I drove to Sophia's flat. The first one in which I mentioned Chloe was just after I'd met her in the Jewel Bar.

Sophia had asked me about my love life, as she usually did.

"I've met someone," I responded.

"Someone special?"

"I think so. She was in a bar, waiting for her friends and I spoke to her because she looked a bit lonely."

"Oh, not because she was gorgeous?"

"No. Gorgeous she is not, but she is clever and interesting, and I like her company. Also, she reminds

me of my Mum."

"Sounds good."

"What about you? Anyone nice around."

"Not really, no- one special. What's your girl's name?"

"Chloe."

"Oh, a good Greek name. Is she Greek?

"No, English, but her surname, De Sanges, is French."

"Chloe de Sanges. I know that name."

"How?"

"At work, I've come across it at work. Can't remember the details, but I'll look her up and let you

know."

"What a coincidence! There can't be many people with that name."

I should have stopped Sophia there and then, not let her check Chloe's name at work. She knew it

was wrong to do that, so did I. The result: that Chloe stood to inherit a fortune was totally mind blowing. I like to think *that it made no difference to me. I liked Chloe from the moment I saw her-*

God knows why some people just click with me; others, even very lovely women, just don't. Soon I loved her- for herself. It did make a difference to Sophia. She encouraged me to date Chloe, then to wed and to bring her to Cyprus. She, I think, believed that she was pulling the strings, as she so often did, with me. My decision to ask Chloe to marry me was mine alone. The Cyprus honeymoon idea

seemed good and got Sophia off my back for a while. However, once we were there she kept contacting me, wanting to meet, even came to the Troodos to see how things were going. That was when I'd told her about Chloe's allergies and the adrenalin pen. She still had a way of worming things out of me. Her voyeurism was as disquieting as her revived attentiveness to me.

Sophia knew that Felicity and Andrei had died and pressed me to get Chloe to the lawyer's office.

Fortunately, that was not a problem as Katherine, Chloe's mother had asked her to do just that. I did not need to say anything and stupidly I omitted to come clean to Chloe about Sophia. I thought Chloe would feel she'd been set up. Of course, Sophia delighted in informing Chloe that she, Sophia, knew all about us. Chloe was surprised when Sophia mentioned the view from our flat in the office. Sophia laughed when telling me that. It made me look so bad.

 I'd hoped that once the legal stuff was sorted Chloe and I could relax and enjoy our honeymoon together. Then came the intrusion into our flat. I realised that our burglar was likely to have been Sophia. I did not know why she came, nor what she was looking for- but now I wonder if it was to remove Chloe's rescue adrenalin pens. My heart sank when I realised that Sophia probably had a master plan: not the one I had envisaged of her being given money by us, but something far more sinister – to kill Chloe, talk me into marrying her and become super – rich.

The drive did not take long. I knew where she lived, having been there on my last visit to Cyprus. I parked the little hire car in the road, went up to the block in which Sophia had an apartment and rang her doorbell. There was no reply. I tried again, not caring if I woke her up.

Still nothing. I wondered what to do. Sophia's flat was on the first floor and had a balcony. I was so angry that I contemplated trying to park the car on the grass beneath, climb onto the roof and thence reach the balcony railings and pull myself up. I'd have done it, had not one of the other residents arrived home just then with a key to the main door. He was a young man, around my age and looked friendly.

"Oh, could you please let me in? I've locked my keys in my flat."

He looked me up and down.

"Which flat?"

"103, that one with the balcony."

"OK."

He opened the main door, I thanked him and ran up the stairs, not wanting to wait with him for the

lift.

I rang the bell outside 103, leaving my hand pressed on it for 30 seconds, the did this again and again. Still no answer. Perhaps Sophia had gone somewhere else after the party? Did she have a

boyfriend that she'd not told me about? My anger increased and I began banging on the door and

shouting her name,

"Sophia, it's Nick. Chloe nearly died. She is in hospital. I know you are in there. Open up."

Suddenly there was the sound of a door being unbolted. I stood facing Sophia's flat, expecting her door to swing open but that noise came from behind me.

An irate old lady stood illuminated in her doorway.

"What do you think you are doing, making such a racket at this time of night? You woke me up."

I turned to face her, preparing a mollifying response, then realised that beneath the hairnet was the face of someone I knew.

"Auntie Theodosia!"

"Nicolaos- is it you?"

I nodded, then hung my head, too embarrassed to speak for a moment. I felt like the little boy she had often looked after in the village, rather than the young man she'd last seen a year ago.

"What on earth is the matter, child?"

That "child" undid me and tears sprang to my eyes. Auntie T, as I called her, could see them in the lights on the landing. She took pity on me.

"You'd better come in."

She pushed her door further open and beckoned me inside. I obeyed, wiping my eyes with the back of my hand. Auntie T led me into the sitting room, where two white cats were asleep on the sofa. She pointed to an armchair.

"Sit down, Nikos. Sit down and tell me all about it."

Sitting opposite me on the small remaining vacant part of the sofa Auntie T leaned forward and looked me in the eye.

"Is it Sophia? What has she done now? Put you in the snake field again?"

I had forgotten that Auntie T had helped me on that occasion, the reminder brought a rush of warmth and gratitude towards her and I began to talk.

"Yes, it's Sophia. You know that I am married now?"

Auntie T nodded.

"Well Sophia came to our celebration party tonight." The awful thought then struck me that Auntie T had not been invited.

"It was only a small affair — at our house," I added hurriedly. "If I'd known you lived here, I'd have

asked you to come too."

"I don't, I'm just cat sitting. Go on."

"She'd made a cake for us, a special one to celebrate our marriage."

I paused, was I going to incriminate Sophia on what was flimsy evidence?

I went on,

"It contained something- pistachios- to which my wife is very allergic. I was, am, very angry and I wanted to talk to Sophia."

"Angry? Why angry Nikos? Upset I could understand."

"I don't know if it was a mistake or not." I was later to regret these words so much.

"Not a mistake?" Auntie T paused. "What exactly do you mean?"

"I told Sophia about Chloe's allergies, she knew about the cashews and pistachios"

"And you think that your cousin would have cold- bloodedly made a cake with them in it to hurt your new wife?".

"I don't know. I don't know, but I wanted to ask her." I put my head in my hands, close to tears.

"Well Nikos, I think that is very unlikely. Anyway, it is far too late to wake up Sophia now. Why don't

you sleep here on the couch then you can speak to her in the morning?"

"Would that be OK?"

"Of course. Wait a minute". Auntie T rose and went to a sideboard covered with bottles.

"These people have so much brandy they won't miss a glass. Here you are it'll help you to sleep."

I took it gratefully from her outstretched hand and sipped its fiery warmth, feeling it spreading down my throat, soothing, calming me.

"Thank you."

"Nikos you are welcome. I am going back to bed now. We will talk more in the morning. Kalinýchta

kalí xekoúrasi."

She turned and left the room, quite regal, despite the hairnet.

I finished the brandy slowly, letting go of the questions crowding my mind, allowing my anger to dissipate. Then I shook off my shoes, lay down on the couch and to my surprise, knew nothing more until the morning.

CHAPTER 26

The next morning I woke early, stiff, and uncomfortable from the sofa. I decided to wake Sophia up to talk to her, so put on my shoes and slipped quietly out of the flat to the door opposite on the landing.

I knocked on that door, quietly at first, then more loudly, all to no avail. Sophia was either dead to the world or simply not there. Auntie T's flat door had closed behind me – so I was now shut out. Not wanting to wake her I slipped down the stairs and left via the front door.   My hire car was in the road where I'd left it; Sophia's little blue sports car was also parked in the street. She must be in the flat- and was too scared to let me in. I drove to the hospital to collect Chloe and found Costas there.

He'd stayed all night. I felt bad about having left but could not explain the reason.

It was a surprise that Chloe wanted to go with Costas to Lefkosia. How could there be still more forms to sign there? I felt hurt and angry again but tried not to show it, covering Chloe with kisses and hugging her tight.

"It's only our honeymoon" was all I allowed myself to say.

When they had gone, I tried Sophia's phone but there was no reply. I spent the morning cleaning up the house, then went for a swim in our new pool. After that tiredness caught up with me and I lay on our bed and had a siesta. I phoned Chloe when I woke, but it went to voicemail and again after my supper of party leftovers. Somewhat disconsolate I went to bed, again alone.

CHAPTER 30

Sophia's story

Always I have loved Nikos, always. Like a brother, then later like a woman loves a man. He was mine to command when little, but now he stands up to me and I like that. What I did not like was his falling in love with a stupid, ugly girl. Hard to see what he saw in her, apart from the money, that is. He says he was drawn to her before ever he knew she would be rich. Well maybe that is true, but the thought of money kept him with her, I am sure. And it was me who found out who she was. Nikos should be grateful, but I know he is angry with me. The man tells me she did not die, he is angry with me too.

What to do? Where to go?

I wish that I had never met the man. He does not tell me his name when we talk, but for sure he in not Frederick Mann as it says on his What's App. The first time I saw him was at lunchtime, the day after the Russian couple- or rather the Russian man and his English wife, had made their wills. He came and sat beside me on the bench where I was eating my lunch. He seemed nice enough then, offering me a cigarette. No good because I don't smoke. He liked that, said I was sensible, then just beggared off. After that he was there a few more times and we began to talk. He was clever, said little about himself, but listened to me. I was pissed off about not getting the raise I'd plucked up the

courage to ask for, he sympathised. Next time he asked if I was interested in earning something on the side.
Interested? Too bloody right I was interested. My car was costing me a fortune in repairs- new tyres needed all round after I must have gone through nails or something.

I wonder?

Just a little information he said. I knew it was wrong, but all he wanted were a couple of addresses.

He could have got them from the phone book, I think- but I gave him them from our files via What's App and he paid me handsomely directly into my bank account. That sorted out the car and I heaved a sigh of relief.

*A week later he was back. This time he seemed less friendly, more pushy. He wanted to know about that couple, where they lived, what the will said. I told him to p*** off. He asked if I wanted my boss to know about last time. I said* *sure, go ahead, tell him. I gave you nothing that wasn't in the phone book anyway. He looked at me hard, then left.*

The next What's App message left me in no doubt – either I got him the information, or my life would become difficult. When you live alone it can be scary at night, odd noises make you jump. Difficult – what did he mean by that? In the end I told him that I'd get him what I could but that was to be the end of it- did we have an agreement? We did.

It turned out that the Limassol address was no longer where they lived. How was that my fault? It was what they'd put down. The will though mentioned other places- including a house at Sea Caves- so he found out about that. There was no peace for the wicked though- he came back wanting to know what had happened as the house was guarded but no-one seemed to be living there. I checked and found that they'd both died of COVID. That'll put an end to this, I thought, but no. He wanted more details of what the will said, who inherited, where the stuff was. That's when the name Chloe de Sanges came up and – lo and behold the same name comes from my lovely Nikos. I hated it and her long before I ever met her. By now the payments were rounding out my bank account nicely, there was no way I could escape from him without beans spilling all over the place. So I played along,

chatted to Nikos on the boring subject of his adoration, so smart, so kind and fed it back to him, not- really- Frederick. He was delighted when Nikos married Chloe and ecstatic that she was coming to Cyprus (Nikos had told me of his honeymoon plans seemingly unaware that I'd put the idea in his head). Men!

Non- Frederick was insistent about something that Chloe had inherited. He said it was the code for a fortune in bitcoin on a USB. Promised to share it with me if I could get hold of the USB. He asked me to search their flat- as if discovered I'd have the excuse that I was trying to visit, to meet Chloe. I didn't ask where the keys came from, just used them to get in and went round it as fast as I could.

There was a handbag hidden under the pillow on the bed- stupid place! I tipped everything out- no USB. There was a syringe though, filled with liquid and covered in diagrams. Light dawned- Nick had mentioned Chloe's severe allergies. This must be her rescue pen. I pocketed it, looked up to make sure no- one had seen me- and saw Nick coming up the steps towards block A.I shoved the stuff under the bed and was out of there in a flash. Think some old biddy from below caught sight of me though.

Frederick's anger at the lack of a USB was mollified by seeing the syringe and hearing what I knew about Chloe's allergies. He took the syringe with him, promising I'd be paid. I was.

His next request made me laugh at first- I had to make a cake for their party. I'd told him that they were having one in our regular What's App chats and that I was invited. Frederick specified the Ottolenghi recipe for a Persian Love cake and it was only when I pulled up the recipe that I understood. My blood ran cold. Sure, I was jealous of her, sure I wanted her out of Nikos' life, but I did not want to kill her. Yet I was more and more afraid of what I'd got into with Mr. Mann. If I didn't make the cake and ensure Chloe ate some my own future was in doubt. He made that clear in his charming, slightly opaque way.

What to do? In the end I made the cake- since it was not certain that Chloe would die. Just a mouthful could not harm her too much, could it?

CHAPTER 31

Nick

Banging noises and barking woke me from a sleep disturbed by frightening dreams of monsters. I sat

up, shook my head, rubbed my eyes, taking time to return to reality. Swinging my legs over the side

of the bed I slipped on my flip flops and stood up, momentarily dizzy. My watch was saying that it

was 10 am. I had overslept, probably because it had taken me ages to get off to sleep. No more siestas!

The noise was coming from the closed front gate to which I hurried. Our guard was standing facing it, trying to fend off two angry- looking policemen standing beside a patrol car. The Alsatian was going crazy.

"What's the matter?" I asked.

"Are you Nikos Nicolaou?"

"Yes."

"Good morning. I am Inspector Grievas and this is Sergeant Charalambous. Please can we come in and speak to you?"

Thinking of the cake, I asked,

"Is it about Sophia, my cousin?"

The policemen looked significantly at each other.

"Yes, sir. Please may we enter?"

I nodded to the guard who opened the gate.

When we were seated in the big light drawing room the Inspector asked,

"You mentioned Sophia. Is that Sophia Nicolaou?"

"Yes, she's my cousin."

"Why did you speak of her?"

"Because she was here on Sunday. She brought a cake to our party, and it nearly killed my wife."

"Aaah. I see. Is that why you were banging on her door on Sunday night?"

"Yes. I was very angry. I wanted to tell her what had happened and for her to know it was her fault."

I stopped there, not wanting to say that it could have been deliberate.

"And what did you say to your cousin when she let you into her flat?"

"She didn't let me in, that's why I was banging on the door. Auntie T heard me and came out of the

flat opposite. She calmed me down and took me in for the night. In the morning I tried Sophia's door

again- but she still didn't answer so I left and went to the hospital to collect my wife."

"Auntie T is Mrs. Theodosia Nicolaou?"

"Yes. Have you spoken to her?"

The Inspector gave a barely perceptible nod.

"I don't want to pursue any action against Sophia. It was an unfortunate accident."

"Have you spoken to Sophia at all since your party?"

"No, when I couldn't see her in person I just gave up. My wife was not keen for me to pursue it."

In fact, Chloe had not spoken to me on the subject- we had skirted round it on our way back from the hospital and then Chloe had left. I still hadn't been able to speak to her on the phone, but I thought/ hoped that this would be her opinion.

"Where is your wife, sir?"

"In Lefkosia. She went with a friend yesterday to sort out some legal matters." Just in time I stopped myself using the word inheritance. I didn't want these chaps thinking I was after Chloe's money.

"Aaah, I see. So, you have been on your own here since then?"

I nodded. There was a pause. I was aware of the distant sound of pebbles being moved by the waves.

The policemen looked at each other.

"Have you entered your cousin's flat at any other time?"

"Yes, I visited her there on my last trip to Cyprus, once or twice. As small children we grew up

together in our village, so we are close, like brother and sister."

"Do you have a key to her flat?"

"No. if I'd had one then I wouldn't have been knocking on the door."

"How did you enter the block without a key?"

"One of the other residents let me in. I said I'd locked myself out."

Now they know I tell lies, I thought.

"Sir what I have to say next may be very upsetting. "

My heart sank, quite literally I felt it skip a beat and become leaden.

"What's happened?"

"I am very sorry to have to inform you that Miss Sophia Nicolaou was found dead in her apartment

earlier today."

My brain was calculating that Sophia must have killed herself in shame at what she'd done to Chloe,

my voice had its own ideas.

"No, no, not Sophia. How? Why?"

"She was found hanged."

My theory was right, the guilt had been too much for Sophia.

"Did she leave a note?"

"Not that we have found."

"Isn't that strange? I thought most suicides left a note"

"As yet sir we are unsure whether this was suicide."

"My God!" Then, as realization dawned. "You don't think that she was murdered?"

The policeman said nothing, just looked at me.

"You don't think that I did it, do you?" The horror of the situation was dawning on me.

"Right now, sir, we are keeping an open mind. Here is my card. Just don't go anywhere without

letting us know. We may wish to question you again."

They rose, as one, to leave. I was unable to move, gobsmacked by events.

"We'll see ourselves out, sir."'

I waved my right hand vaguely in a gesture of I'm not sure what. Suddenly an important question

came to mind.

"When did Sophia die?"

The Inspector turned round,

"We are awaiting information about that, sir. The young lady was only found earlier this morning.

I am very sorry for your loss."

This unexpected expression of sympathy undid me and I began to sob involuntarily in a way I last did

as a child: shaking, chest heaving, gasps, tears flowing down my hand- covered face. I was unaware

of the departure of the police or of the sympathetic howling of the dog. How long this lasted I don't

know, but eventually it stuttered to a stop and I was left exhausted, both physically and emotionally.

My mind was still refusing to accept what my heart knew: Sophia dead? No, not Sophia, so full of

energy and life, not her. There must be some mistake. Perhaps recent events were a play, "The

Inspector Calls Again", intended as a bad joke. Gradually reality took over. Sophia had probably hung

herself- but why? Even if she had been guilty of deliberately provoking Chloe's anaphylaxis the Sophia

I knew would have toughed it out, denied it, not killed herself. So why? My brain whirred. Was

someone else involved?

 I knew one thing though- I needed to speak to Chloe. I rang her mobile again and was highly relieved when it was answered.

"Hello Nick! Sorry I missed your calls- my phone ran out of battery, and I forgot to bring the charger-

I'm in a shop in Limassol buying one and they've let me plug it in."

"Hi sweetheart! Oh, I am so happy to hear your voice my darling. I have missed you so much."

It was true. I had begun to feel incomplete without her around.

"That's nice. I've missed you too. I'll be home in a couple of hours- just have to find the bus station.

Could you pick me up in Paphos at the bus station there?"

"Of course, love. What time?"

"Three o'clock according to the timetable."

"See you then my darling. I have things to tell you."

"So have I. Love you, bye"

She cut off the call before I could reciprocate. I hoped it was because she was in a public place. Then I

began to fret about her safety. If Sophia had been – murdered- the word was not easy to use even in

my thoughts- perhaps because Chloe had not died, then whoever wanted Chloe dead might try again.

I thought of rushing to collect her from Limassol, but rejected this as she'd have to wait somewhere

for me- she'd be safer on a public bus. I must be at the Paphos bus station in good time, so she did not

have to hang around there.

Why would someone want Chloe dead? The inheritance was the obvious answer. I sensed that there

was more to it than I'd been told. A cold dread possessed me- from all those stories of tainted money

and jewels causing havoc down generations. What if Chloe died? Presumably it would all land on me.

That thought made the dread worse. What if the police thought I had put Sophia up to it, then killed her so she did not talk? I had no alibi from the time Chloe and Costas left until the police arrived- except of course for the guard who would know if I'd gone out. Thank goodness we hadn't got rid of him immediately as we'd been tempted to do.

An even worse idea then surfaced. What if Chloe also thought that I was the villain, using Sophia to kill her and inherit her wealth? She now knew that through Sophia I'd been aware of the possible windfall when we married. Perhaps that's why she went to Lefkosia with Costas. Bloody, bloody, bloody hell! How could I convince Chloe that I love her for her, not for her money?

Again, my head went into my hands. What on earth could I do?

CHAPTER 32

We arrived in Nicosia mid-afternoon and went straight to Costas' apartment. From there he rang Ti who was at work in the Embassy, but who agreed to come round for supper. Costas was all for ordering in a take- away, but I wanted to impress Ti with my culinary skills and so searched the kitchen cupboards for something to cook. There was not much to find. Costa, seeing how much I wanted to make a meal offered to go out and buy stuff if I gave him a shopping list. I said I'd go too, but he dissuaded me on the grounds of my recent spell in hospital without much sleep.

"Chloe, you should lie down and rest for a couple of hours, then you'll enjoy the evening more."

He was right, of course. I checked my phone for the recipe, then wrote a list.

"Here you are, just don't add any pistachios to it!"

Off he went and I took the opportunity to lie horizontal on the sofa (one of the advantages of being short) and meditate. The Buddha lotus position just does not work for me. It took a while for my mind to settle. Once it did, I felt wonderfully peaceful, calm and content having accepted my miniscule role in life, the universe and everything. Away from Nick and the powerful attraction he held for me I could think logically about the future. I loved him and I should stay with him and trust him completely. If it was my fortune he wanted to inherit, then no doubt he would simply leave me now that I had arranged its disposal elsewhere in the event of my death. Time would tell. I fell

asleep.

Costas returned and I woke and began making chicken yakitori, something I know Ti likes. I asked Costas to help by making a salad for our starter. As instructed, he'd bought a pudding (my skills are savoury rather than sweet). We chatted amiably while we worked and then sat down with a cup of tea when all was more or less ready.

I asked Costas why he lived in the city when he could work anywhere with his computer. He replied that he was a city person, liking the ease of shopping, eating drinking, and not minding the noise and the traffic. In London he'd been very happy in Queen's Park where he'd had the convenience of a city but also some open green space nearby.

Ti arrived while we were still drinking tea. She had brought a bottle of wine and some flowers- or rather a plant, with her.

"For you, Costas," she said." It'll clean the air in your flat."

I thought the sentiment might have been better expressed, but Costas seemed delighted.

"Hello my darling, " Ti came and gave me a hug. "How are you? How is married life?"

"Wonderful Ti, you should……." I was going to say try it sometime, then I remembered Andrei- and altered the sentence to " you should know."

Ti did not appear to have noticed that stumble. Costas spoke up,

"Chloe had anaphylaxis again." Ti had been around for many of the early episodes.

"Oh, not again! You poor thing, what happened?"

Costas took it upon himself to explain and I added details of which he was unaware- such as Sophia

making absolutely sure that I ate some of the cake.

Ti looked grave. "I should have warned you, Chloe. I am so sorry- but we only received some information on Friday."

"About what?" I was defensive, hoping it did not concern Nick.

"Sophia has been meeting a man who is known to work for the Russians."

"What?"

"It came as a surprise to me too. I'd been thinking of her as a simple secretary who might be in

cahoots with your husband, her cousin- not as a bigger player. It was a long shot that I suggested

surveillance on her, largely because you told me that she was related to Nick and knew about the

will. I asked for it largely to protect you. It took a while to get it through the right channels- but once

it began we found that she has been getting money fairly regularly from the Russians."

"What for?"

"Probably related to the USB. The stuff that has emerged so far could have come from elsewhere- so

the Russkies are not sure whether you have it or not and if you do whether you have any idea of its

contents. The burglaries at your flat were likely to have been them searching for it."

"So I am still not safe? I thought once the Putin stuff came out they'd know the USB was in the hands of MI6, or 5 or whatever."

"No, I was wrong."

Ti took my face into her hands and looked me straight in the eye. "Chloe please believe me when I say that I am desperately, desperately sorry to have involved you in this. I would not have done it for the world."

"Why does the bloody USB matter so much?"

"It matters more than I knew. Not only does it have evidence against Putin, but there is also a coded

message which was only broken today. I can't say very much, but it is seriously big stuff and vital to our future and interests in Cyprus and the Middle East."

"Why try to kill me?"

"Not sure, but with you dead Sophia could have persuaded a grieving Nick to let her deal with your

stuff – and would have been able to look hard for that bloody USB, as you call it. Removing you

would also stop you from passing it on to someone- your grandfather for example- if you did have it.

Putin's Russians deal with people like chess pieces, knocking them off the board when it suits them"

"Does this mean that Nick is in the clear?"

"I can't say for sure, but it looks more like individual enterprise on Sophia's part. If she'd wanted to

get rid of you to have a rich Nick for herself why would she bother with the Russians?"

My heart didn't just leap, it somersaulted with joy.

"I always knew Nick is not a bad man. Thank God you can see that too now."

I stood up and hugged Ti. Our differences over Nick had pushed a wedge between us for a while, now it was gone we could spring back into happy alignment.

"What should I do now? Am I still a target?" I asked.

"From tonight I think that you will be safe. Something will happen which will reveal knowledge that must have come from Andrei and therefore from the USB. They will know we have it and that there is no point in going after you."

"Not even in revenge? Look at the Skripals."

"That was for what they saw as betrayal; you have not betrayed anyone."

"I hope that's true. Let's have supper, come and sit down."

We spent the meal chatting about other things, Ti telling us of a film she'd seen "The Tragedy of Macbeth", Costas decrying the violence in the Coen brothers' oeuvre. I didn't mention that the original Shakespeare play was pretty violent. In fact, I had little to contribute as my life was full of Nick and not much else, funny how one's horizons narrow in an intense relationship. Presumably not for ever. I wanted to see if Nick had called, so surreptitiously got out my phone under the table. It

refused to light up- battery flat. I'd have to charge it when I went to bed and ring him then. Keen to do that, I hurried the entry of the pudding , a cheesecake which was delicious, especially when combined with the Greek (for Greek read Turkish) coffee which accompanied it, courtesy of Costas.

Then, pleading tiredness I took myself off to my allotted bedroom, which I was soon going to have to share with Ti again. I threw my hastily packed bag on the bed, searching among its contents for my charger. It was not there. Carefully I picked up everything and put items back one by one. Still no charger. Damn! I knew that both Ti and Costas used iPhones and so would not have an android charger.

Nick my darling I am sending you much love by telepathy- I hope you receive it. I thought hard.

Then I climbed into bed feeling thwarted and cross, so unsurprisingly was still awake when Ti joined me. She did not speak as I was lying still with my eyes closed, but when I turned over and opened them, she said,

"I thought you were asleep."

"No, I'm too cross with myself. I forgot my charger and can't ring Nick."

"You can use my phone."

"Only one problem- I don't know his number off by heart. There's no landline in your house."

"God, it's crazy how reliant we are on those mobile gadgets, isn't it?"

"Too right. I can buy a charger in Limassol tomorrow. It'd be good to have a spare then I could leave

one in my suitcase."

She went off to the bathroom and I settled down again to try to sleep.

CHAPTER 33

Costas and I set off early the next morning. He had an appointment to keep, and I was keen to get back to Nick. I bought the charger, and we had a brief phone conversation, arranging that he'd pickme up from the Paphos bus station. I didn't tell him about Sophia and the Russians, I thought it would be better to be with him when I did so, then I could gauge his reactions. Despite my protestations to Ti, I still felt the need to be absolutely certain about Nick.

I needn't have worried. You know the song, "It's in his kiss"? Well, it was. Back in his arms I had no doubts at all about his love for me, nor of mine for him. We clung to each other as if we'd been apart for weeks.

"No PDAs allowed in the bus station", he said. "Let's go home sweetheart."

Once in the car Nick's mood seemed to change. He sighed and confided,

"I have some bad news, I'm afraid."

"Oh, God, what's happened?"

"Sophia is dead."

I was hocked and shorrified as Ti used to say.

"What? Sophia? Oh, Nick, I am so sorry. How did it happen? When?"

"The police don't know yet- or they may do by now but they haven't told me- but it was sometime between when she came home from our party and yesterday morning. She was found hanging, they are not sure if it was suicide or if she was killed."

Nick looked down, shutting his eyes briefly. I offered to drive but was refused.

"Chloe, I have more to tell you. It's easier to do while I'm driving. After you were resuscitated I left you in the hospital and went to Sophia's flat- I was so angry about what she had done to you and I wanted to find out if it was an accident or not. She didn't answer the door. My old aunt was staying in the flat opposite- she heard the racket I was making, shouting and banging on Sophia's door. She took me in, calmed me down and let me sleep there. In the morning I got up early and tried Sophia's door again- still no reply so I came back to you in the hospital."

"I wondered why you left me."

"I'm sorry. I knew you were OK and thought Costas would stay- I just had to tackle Sophia

immediately."

"So, you don't know if she was not answering or if she was already dead?"

"Yes. The police came round yesterday to question me. I think they will believe Auntie T, but if

Sophia died while you were away in Lefkosia then I have no alibi."

"Of course, you could have been very clever- got in with a key, murdered Sophia, left the wiped key inside and then banged on the door."

"Yes, I guess the police have thought of that."

"Well, I have news for you which might help."

"What?"

"Sophia was seen chatting to a Russian and has been getting money paid into her account."

"How does that help? "

I realized that Nick knew nothing of Andrei's activities and the USB, still less that Ti was alive.

"I have a lot to tell you love. Unlike you, doing so whilst we are driving does not suit me. Let's get in the house, make a cup of tea and I'll come clean."

That is what we did. I took my time and explained about Ti's foray into espionage, Andrei's retaining secrets as protection and the fate of the USB. Nick was very angry at first that I'd kept him in the dark about Ti and the spy connection, but did say that the second burglary, after which he'd been told not to enter the flat, did put him in mind of the Salisbury poisonings and he'd begun to wonder.

When I'd finished, he asked,

"So, you don't own this house if Ti is still alive, you are not a rich heiress?"

"Probably not."

"Thank goodness Chloe! I could not be more delighted. I want to support you- and I hope our children- myself. I hated the idea of being a kept man."

"That my darling, is music to my ears."

Later that evening we were sitting companionably on the sofa watching the BBC News. There was

an item about the sudden resignation of the Foreign Secretary.

"That's it, that's it! I bet that's what Ti meant."

Nick looked puzzled.

"The stuff on the USB- some of it was coded top secret very important stuff that Andrei was bringing

with him. Ti said it would come out soon and then I would be safe because the Russians would know

that the USB had reached the right place and I no longer had it hidden away somewhere."

"You think Andrei had something on our Foreign Secretary?"

"Yes, perhaps she was a mole, planted long ago." Rather a mixed metaphor even for me.

"Well, I'll be damned. I thought that sort of thing only happened in John le Carre novels."

I laughed." Perhaps we are in a novel and don't know it."

"We are in a honeymoon if you remember. Bedtime, Mrs Nicolaou."

CHAPTER 34

I hope that I can hang on to the memory of last night until I die. That's all I 'm prepared to say about it.

Next morning the Cyprus Police rang, asking Nick to go down to the Paphos station to make a statement. He wanted to go alone, but I insisted upon accompanying him to ensure fair play.

Both of us felt nervous, goodness knows what it must be like if you are guilty.

Entering the place was not easy. We had to park nearby then walk to the gate which was locked, ring the bell and be admitted to the courtyard, then the same palaver with the front door of the building.

The police obviously did not feel very safe. Once inside there was a reception desk to which we reported and were then asked to wait. We sat on hard plastic chairs. I wished we'd had the sense to have breakfast before coming, but Nick had wanted to get it over with as soon as he could.

"Do you want coffee?" I asked him.

He nodded." That would be good, thanks love."

I asked at the reception desk if I could go and fetch 2 coffees but was told no food or drink could be

consumed in the waiting room.

"You go then love, get yourself some coffee and breakfast, then come back for me."

"Are you sure?"

"Yes, I'll be fine."

So off I went. It was a mistake.

When I returned half an hour later, having stored a coffee and a croissant for Nick in the car, he was nowhere to be seen. I sat down to wait and opened the paperback I'd also bought at a local charity shop and began to read. Chapter 1 was finished and there was still no sign of Nick. I stood up, stretched and moved to the desk, where a cup of coffee was prominently displayed. I spoke to the person at the desk.

"Is there some way of finding out how long my husband will be in here?"

He looked up from under his bushy eyebrows.

"What is his name?"

"Nicolaos Nicolaou."

I'll check, he picked up the phone and pressed one button. A brief conversation in Greek followed, incomprehensible to me. He put down the receiver.

"Your husband is still in the interrogation suite at the moment, but he is being transferred to the cells."

"What?"

"Someone will come and speak to you soon. Please sit down."

CHAPTER 35

Nick

The phone call from the police was unwelcome, but not unexpected. I thought the statement would

be a formality now that there was evidence of Sophia's Russian involvement and encouraged Chloe

to get dressed so we could go into Paphos, get it done and then have brunch somewhere nice.

At the Police Station the Fort Knox- type entry measures were a tad off – putting, as was the lack of

warmth in the Receptionist's welcome. Hey though, I thought, this is the Police, not Hotel California! I

wish my mind had not conjured up that comparison, I had wanted to use something like the Ritz, but

Hotel California came to mind. Perhaps some part of my brain realised what was coming.

It was about 15 minutes after Chloe left to get some coffee that they finally called me into an interview room. Naively I didn't think to ask if I should have a lawyer present. They were just going to

write down the same stuff that I'd told them before and then I'd sign it, as far as I was concerned.

It was disconcerting to sit across a table from two officers, one male, one female, who introduced

themselves politely. I immediately forgot both their names. The lady started a tape recorder and

spoke the date, time, who was present. She cautioned me, then began to question me: how I knew

Sophia, how well I knew her, what was her reaction to my recent marriage, then about Chloe, similar

questions, including how did she react to Sophia? The male officer sympathised with my being

squeezed between two women, both of whom wanted me.

"It wasn't like that!"

"Tell us what it was like."

I explained that Sophia and I were never romantically involved, but like brother and sister.

"So why did you spend the night at her flat last week?"

How did they know?

"My wife had to go to the British Embassy in Lefkosia on a legal matter- it was at the last minute so

she could not pick me up from the Mall as we'd arranged. I had no car and was wondering what to

do- then I thought of Sophia. She loves shopping- so I suggested she come and get me when she

finished work, we'd have a look round, get a meal, then she could drop me back at the Airbnb flat.

When we got there the front door was open and it had been burgled- ransacked."

"Did you report this to the police?"

"No. I spoke to Chloe and she took advice from someone, then said leave it alone and go to a hotel

for tonight. We'd sort it out together next day."

"And you obeyed?" He sounded incredulous.

"Yes. I was tired, in no mood to hang around for the police to arrive, so I just closed the door and left

with Sophia in her car. She offered me her couch for the night, and I accepted, preferring that to

trailing round the hotels trying to find one with a room free."

"Did you tell your wife this?"

"No, I let her think that I stayed in an hotel."

"Because?"

"Because she would have preferred that."

"So, Mr Nicolaou, you admit that you tell lies when it suits you?"

"Don't we all?"

It was at this point that light dawned. They were trying to stitch me up for Sophia's killing. I

remembered my rights.

"I am not willing to continue with this until I have a lawyer present."

That took a while. The only legal name that I knew was Mr Antoniades, but he could not help as he was involved as Sophia's employer. I ended up with the duty solicitor, a very young- looking guy. I hoped he was savvy despite his lack of experience We had a quick chat. I told him everything I knew.

He seemed fazed but took copious notes. We were called back to the interview room.

"So, Mr Nicolaou, you spent the night with your cousin without your wife's knowledge?"

"Yes, but it was innocent."

"So why not tell your wife?"

"Chloe would have been upset. Unnecessarily as it happens."

"So there was friction between them?"

"To an extent yes. It started badly because I had not told Chloe that Sophia worked for the lawyer

that Chloe was going to see."

"About what?"

"Her aunt's will."

"Her aunt is Cypriot?"

"I don't think so, but she was living in Cyprus when she died."

The questions went on and on. At no point did the young solicitor stop me. The facts came out:

Sophia knew about the will, she knew Chloe's unusual name when I mentioned it, she knew that Chloe might be very rich one day."

"So your cousin told you that your then girlfriend might be an heiress?"

The young man next to me put his hand on my arm.

"No comment," he said. He saw, as I did, where this was leading. Sophia informs me about Chloe's

possible fortune, we cook up a plot that I marry her, we bump her off then share the proceeds- but

when the plot fails, I bump Sophia off so she cannot spill the beans.

How to convince them otherwise? I remembered what Chloe had told me.

"Sophia was meeting with a Russian intelligence officer. He was paying her for something, probably

information. There was something to which Chloe had access that they wanted desperately and were

prepared to kill for. That's why we were burgled."

Even to my ears it sounded unlikely.

"Do you have any evidence to back up these wild allegations, Mr Nicolaou?"

"No, but my wife and her aunt can tell you more,"

"The dead aunt?" they both laughed.

"Yes, she's not really dead. Just had to pretend to avoid Putin's henchmen."

"You have a vivid imagination, sir."

"Let's go to the night of your cousin's murder. I believe you said previously that you went to her flat?"

"No comment. I refuse to say any more until you have spoken to my wife."

"Where is she?"

"Waiting for me here, I think."

The two interrogators looked at each other and nodded.

The tape was spoken to again with the time and the fact that the interview was concluded.

"Sir, we will speak to your wife now if she is available. In the meantime we would like for you not to

be in contact with her, so will hold you in the cells."

"The cells?" I was horrified, scared too.

"Yes sir, you remain a suspect and we have the right to hold you for a few hours whilst we investigate

further." He pressed a buzzer and the door opened. A young policeman came and took hold of my arm, getting me to rise and move towards the door.

I looked back. "I am innocent, you know."

"They all say that, sir." The "sir" was said with deliberate contempt. They obviously thought I was as

guilty as hell. Chloe, please do your best to save me, I thought, sending that message, I hoped, through the ether to her brain.

CHAPTER 36

Someone did come to speak to me very soon. She invited me politely to come and answer some questions as my husband had indicated that I might further their enquiry. I agreed willingly, thinking that I could help Nick.

The policewoman took me to a room with a desk where two other officers were sitting. I was motioned to the chair opposite. It was slightly warm.

Nick was in here, I thought.

The two looked at each other significantly when they saw me. I could tell that they were thinking

that Nick must have married me for my money.

The initial questions were easy- who I was, my relationship to Nick, my knowledge of Sophia. Then

came ones about my allergies and the anaphylaxis. I tried to be as objective as possible but found myself gabbling on because I was nervous.

"Your husband knew about this allergy of yours?"

"Yes, I told him a few days ago on our honeymoon. I'd almost forgotten about it until I tasted baklava. It gave me lip tingling, a warning sign, so I knew that I couldn't eat it. Then I had to explain to Nick. I showed him my adrenalin pen and how to use it in case there were any further incidents. The food here is different, you know. More hidden nuts."

"And yet you ate the cake?"

"Only a mouthful. It was stupid of me- but I'd had a few drinks, so my defences were down."

"And that was enough to nearly kill you?"

Yes, it's an amazingly powerful reaction. If Costas hadn't given me adrenalin, I doubt I'd be here to talk to you."

"So, your husband did not give the adrenalin, although you had taught him to do so?"

"He couldn't find it in my handbag, I think it was taken when our flat was burgled the first time."

The whole saga of the burglary came out, including the fact that my neighbour had seen a young lady in a blue sports car, who could have been Sophia.

"So your husband knew you would need one of those adrenalin pens in the event of anaphylaxis – and you think his cousin Sophia removed it from your handbag before giving you cake laced with pistachios?"

I realised how bad this was looking for Nick.

"Yes, but Sophia had other reasons to burgle us. I think she was looking for something else, a USB.

She didn't find it and then we were burgled again soon after- but this time the whole place was completely turned over."

"What it this USB? It is the first time it has been mentioned."

"I don't know how much I am allowed to tell you. Please could I make a phone call?"

"To your solicitor?"

"No, to my aunt."

"Is this the aunt who is dead?" His eyebrows raised as he said this. I was alarmed that he knew, but did not confirm it, just said,

"My aunt Felicity. She is in the British Embassy here."

"Very well."

"I need to use the internet, is that possible?"

"You can make an ordinary phone call."

"No, I can't. The only way I can contact her is if the call is encrypted."

They looked at each other. There was conversation in Greek, the lady shrugged her shoulders and said,

"Very well. I will get you the password, come with me."

She led me to an office where there was a router on the desk.

"The password is on there. I'll wait outside."

"Thank you."

I logged on and rang Ti via Signal.

"Hi love, how are you?" she answered the call.

"Not good, Ti. I am in a police station where Nick is being held in the cells. They obviously think he killed Sophia after putting her up to murder me for my money. I need to explain about Andrei and

you and the USB and the Russians, but I don't know what is safe to say. I don't want to get you into trouble."

"Sweetheart, thank you. I'll speak to them and sort this out. Can you put one of them on?"

I opened the door to find the policewoman just behind it.

"Please could you speak to my aunt?"

There followed a long conversation, one end of which I heard. This was mostly monosyllabic.

"Yes"

"Where?"

"When?"

"How much?"

"I see."

Then,

"We will need proof of these allegations. Can you supply it?"

Obviously Ti had said yes because a minute or so later the woman was looking hard at photos and documents sent via the link.

"Would you be willing to come here and make a statement?"

This time the answer was no- but I gathered that an arrangement was made for a police visit inside

the Embassy (where Ti had diplomatic immunity and was safe from Russians and from prosecution for her undeath) for the purposes of a statement.

"Thank you."

The phone was handed back to me, and the policewoman left the office.

"Oh Ti, thank you so much. "

"My darling, I think it will do the trick. We have evidence of Sophia's contact entering the block of

flats earlier that night. Presumably he waited in there for her to come home, then he must somehow have got information that you had not died. I guess he was angry with Sophia and thought she was a

risk if left alive to talk."

"Or perhaps he was going to kill her anyway?"

"I doubt it. I think the idea would have been to encourage a relationship with Nick, then they'd get the USB and access to both the funds and the information that way."

I thanked her again and we said goodbye and promised to keep each other up to date.

CHAPTER 37

The policewoman took me back to the waiting room- and to my intense joy Nick was there, waiting for me.

I hurried to him, and we hugged tightly.

"Thank God, they let you go," I said.

"Chlo, you came up trumps, my darling, thank you, thank you." he kissed the top of my head.

"Were you scared?"

"Too damn right I was. It is horrible in those cells. If ever I contemplated a life of crime being stuck in

there for a while would have put me off. Let's go home, love. We've only got a few days left of our honeymoon."

Three weeks had seemed such a long, indulgent time- but it had gone so quickly, far too fast for my liking. A thought struck me.

"Will we be allowed to leave? Or are you still a suspect?"

"I don't know. They didn't say anything."

"It would be quite nice to have to stay on for a while."

"Sure, there's more that I want to show you. I haven't taken you up to the village yet for one thing. I

will have to go there and see Eleni and Demetrios to say how sorry I am about Sophia. Would you

like to come with me?"

"I'm not sure. I might be in the way. I hardly knew Sophia and then there was the cake incident…."

"I understand. I'll go on my own the first time, but you should come with me to the funeral,

whenever that can be held. Usually it is done quickly, but I guess it depends on the police."

"Should we alter our flight back to a later date? Or do you have to get back for work?"

"I have a couple of meetings scheduled for next week, nothing vital and I could make them virtual, I suppose. I'll check when were back in the house if that's possible."

I was delighted, made up, as they say. Not only would it give us more time together here it might also convince the police of his innocence if Nick did not hurry back to the UK.

In the event we awarded ourselves another two weeks in Cyprus. First, we visited the village where Nick and Sophia grew up. I decided to be brave and go with Nick. It was not the homecoming with his bride that he had planned and I could see he wanted my support. There was an understandable pall of sadness hanging over the place at the loss of one of the village's daughters. Aunt Eleni and Uncle Demetrios were hollow-eyed and tearful, Nick having brought back memories of Sophia's childhood. Nick hugged them, crying too. I was about to offer my hand to Eleni, wondering how she felt about me now, but switched the gesture to a warm hug instead. It was reciprocated. They did not blame me or Nick for what had happened, but Demetrios said,

"Oh Nick, I wish we could go back to when you were here. If you had stayed perhaps things would have been different. Sophia might have been less headstrong, wilful. She might be alive now. Such a waste, such a waste of life, a beautiful life, my daughter, my Sophie." He turned away to hide his tears.

"I believe that we will see our daughter again," Aunt Eleni tried to smile, but burst into fresh tears.

We had coffee with them, gave them the plant which we had brought as a gift, then went for a walk around the village. The houses were of stone, close quartered, with narrow streets between them.

A donkey was carrying a load of sticks, led by an old lady in black. Every bit of land was put to use, chickens here, crops there, fig trees, lemon trees, walnuts. No bananas though, it gets too cold up in the hills.

Nick showed me the field where Sophia threw the doll for him to fetch.

"Are there still snakes?" I asked.

"Probably," he said. "The farmers still wear high boots, carry a stick and beat the ground in front of

them before they tread because of the eight species of snake on this island, three are venomous, but

only one is dangerous to humans. That one is the blunt nosed viper."

"Is it a small one, the small ones are usually the dangerous ones, aren't they? "

"No, it's a fairly big fat snake, up to 2 metres long, silvery grey in colour. They like water and sometimes end up in swimming pools in summer."

"Ugh!" I shuddered at the thought of encountering one in our pool.

"Too cool now for that," Nick was reassuring.

"Let's go home," I said, "it's dangerous here."

CHAPTER 38

We had to go back though a few days later. The police had released Sophia's body for burial and we were expected to attend the various ceremonies of the Greek Orthodox rite. I knew from my theology course that there were five stages in a Greek Orthodox funeral: a wake, which starts the day before the funeral, the funeral service, a burial ceremony, a post funeral luncheon, then a memorial service a week later. The strong faith of the community in life after death and the reunion of the soul with the body and with Christ means that cremation is forbidden.

Sophie's body had been prepared by the funeral home in Paphos but was brought to her family house where her wake took place. To my intense relief the coffin was not open, contrary to the usual practice. I guessed that Sophie's appearance probably precluded that. The priest was there praying. Nick whispered to me that he repeated the phrase "Holy God, HolyMighty, Holy Immortal, have mercy on us," three times. Then various people spoke, apparentlysaying good things about Sophia. I found it impossible to understand their words and was relieved when Nick said we could decently leave.

Beatrice Epstein messaged me on the way home. The police had found fingerprints on Sophia that were not Nick's and there was an alert out for the Russian. She felt that we were all safe now the USB contents had put paid to the career of the UK Foreign Secretary and the police were looking elsewhere for Sophia's killer. She'd like to meet Nick. Was that possible?

He was not exactly enthusiastic about becoming acquainted with the woman who had tried to

poison his wife's mind against him. I reminded him that Ti was also the reason for our current

luxurious lifestyle, but that cut little ice. However, he did agree to meet her.

I replied in the affirmative, suggesting a date next week. I might have known that this would not do for my impulsive relative.

"Great- I'll come to yours tomorrow" appeared on my screen.

By this time we were entering the house so I was able to use the internet to call Ti and let her know that we'd be at Sophia's funeral tomorrow. She asked if she could join us as she felt some responsibility for what had happened to that poor girl. If she and Andrei had gone to another solicitor Sophia would still be alive.

"Tell her no," said Nick when I consulted him. "It is not appropriate."

Ti said she understood- but that she'd like to call in anyway early in the morning before we left for the village. She had important things to discuss with us that could involve Sophia. We agreed to this and tidied the house quickly before getting gratefully into bed.

True to her word Ti was with us for breakfast, having brought a bottle of whisky for the guard and a bone for the dog. She sized Nick up whilst offering an elbow in COVID-approved fashion.

"Chloe, I believe you have chosen the handsomest man in Cyprus."

Nick laughed, not totally immune to such outrageous flattery.

"A pleasure to meet my first zombie."

Of course, they got on like a house on fire. I hadn't needed the worry that had again spoiled my sleep.

We sat round a table on the balcony for breakfast and Ti explained her ideas.

"There is a fortune in bitcoin on that USB, far more than anyone needs. It's probably dirty money, but we'll never be able to give it back to the right people. I'd like to suggest that we share enough between us to invest so that we can live on the interest, then use the rest to make a Charitable Foundation. We can work for that. It could be named after Andrei and Sophia too if you like. We can decide on its mission between us. My vote would be for refugees."

Nick thought for a moment then said,

"That is a terrific idea. I'll ask Eleni and Demetrios what they would like. My vote would be for combatting climate change and environmental destruction."

I seconded this and pointed out that those aims coincided because there would probably be lots of climate change refugees.

"We could run it ourselves- or have a Board of Trustees," Ti explained.

"Let's get legal advice," Nick replied, very sensibly I thought. Ti did too

"Good idea."

Our excitement generated a mood of concord and happiness- only broken when Nick remembered

that we had a funeral to attend.

"We should go now. Ti, why don't you come with us?"

This was such a reversal that I was astonished. Obviously, Ti had made a good impression on my husband.

"If you think it would be OK, then I'd like that."

I found myself, slightly sniffily, saying,

"You need to wear black. I've only got the one dark dress that we bought specially."

"No problem. I have a dark jacket in the car and my trousers are black anyway."

So off we went, in Ti's Land Rover as it was bigger than the Suzuki, up the hill to the village, bearingthe white roses picked from our garden.

The little Byzantine church was set on the edge of the village, with fields beyond in a long valley.

Beyond that were further hills, gradually increasing in height, more valleys, until the Troodos mountains were reached. It was a peaceful spot and I felt that Sophia was coming home, too soon perhaps, but she would be in the right place. I hoped Nick felt the same.

Outside the church was of pale stone in a Greek cross shape with a rounded end and a central Dome. Inside was very plain, apart from a small area high in the dome where some paint remained, possibly of God the Creator. Beneath this lay Sophie's coffin, facing east, feet towards the altar. The priest was already intoning prayers and there was a chest -tightening quantity of incense in the air.

 Everyone remained standing, listening to the priest, occasionally joining in the singing. I could not

come to terms with the thought that Sophie, a living, breathing person so recently, was actually inside that box. It was my first funeral and I found it terrifying. That terror and the incense combined

with the dusty interior did bad things to my asthma and I had to get outside. Unfortunately, I was not

close to the door and had to make my way there, dodging round people, saying,"Parakalo," as what I hoped was an apology. One lady put her finger to her lips, motioning me to be quiet.

Once outside in the porch I found my blue inhaler and took a couple of puffs. Gradually breathing became less difficult. I peeped back inside and saw that people were moving around the coffin now, each depositing a flower upon it, before making their way to the door. I stepped back and waited for Ti and Nick to emerge.

CHAPTER 39

Sophie's burial was to be in the Orthodox cemetery, close
by the church. We mourners waited outside the church
while the funeral director's men brought out the coffin on
their shoulders. In their free hand they each held some of
the flowers which had been strewn over it. Then we walked
sorrowfully behind it to the burial ground. Nick took the
opportunity to greet Eleni and Demetrios and to take a
tearful Aunt Theo's arm on the short journey. Ti and I
walked together at the back, also arm in arm. Ti looked
downcast and I could imagine that she was thinking of
Andrei. I wondered what kind of funeral he had? Did Ti
even know? I squeezed her arm.

"Bless you Chlo," she said.

The cemetery was in a beautiful open spot, with hills
around. Now it was midday the sun was strong

 overhead and I was sweating in my dark, long -sleeved
dress. Ti and I stood at the back, allowing

family and neighbours to be closer to the grave into which
the coffin was lowered while the priest continued praying.

"Wonderful spot, I'd like to end up somewhere like this," I said.

"Me too," responded Ti, "and we probably can."

I was too short to see much of what was happening so my attention wandered and I gazed out at the surrounding countryside, thinking that when my time came I would want to be in just such a place. High in the sky a bird was wheeling in circles, gaining height. Buteo buteo, I remembered its name. Nick had shown me the common buzzard over the Paphos plains a few days ago and I recognized the dark wing tips and barred tail. I wondered if he had seen it. A flash of light from the far hill caught my eye, probably another birdwatcher with binoculars. I bent forward to peer between the folk in front to see what Nick was doing. Ti pulled suddenly on my arm and I turned to her, in time to see the shock on her face as she slipped to the ground, dead.

For the second time in my life Ti caused me to faint.

EPILOGUE

The Russian marksman was caught when he tried to leave Cyprus. An island makes escape that much harder, even when you have ships with doubtful origins coming and going. He was found in a container of one bound for Istanbul. He admitted to killing both Sophia and Ti in return for a diminution in his sentence. He probably had some useful information to impart too.

We buried Ti with her beloved Andrei in the cemetery near our house. My parents and grandparents came for the funeral, all upset- but most of them had already grieved for her fake demise and so were less fazed than they might have been, except for Grandpa who was visibly aged and saddened. I suspect he felt guilty. They took the opportunity to take a look at us, Cyprus and our house. All seemed in order, and they left content with my situation.

Nick and I decided to remain in Cyprus. I cannot be certain that I am safe, but it is easier to protect oneself here and again the fact that it is an island means that those coming in can be monitored. Like Andrei before me I hope for regime change in Russia. Money is not a problem. My inheritance is sufficient to allow us to live here comfortably and idly for the rest of our days on the interest alone. Nick though insists on working and continues his business from here, with the aid of a London cousin. There is apparently no problem in gaining residency. We speak often with my grandparents on Signal as we set up the Charity Foundation in Sophia, Ti and Andrei's names. It will largely deal with combatting climate change and aiding those made refugees because of it. It seems a fitting tribute to my beloved aunt and her much -loved husband and I hope that they are at peace together.

Who knows why one person is attracted to another? Psychologists may, but certainly not me, but I have an idea that when Nick saw me that first evening in the Jewel Bar he was subconsciously reminded of his mother. Photos show her as short, not beautiful, but with a kind, intelligent face- that's how I like to think of myself. Funny how the fact that he took pity on me then resulted in this whole episode – and in the death of Sophia. I do feel guilty that she is dead because of me. Nick, I know does too and it casts a small shadow across the happiness we share. Happy we are though, here in Cyprus which flirted with winter for a few days in January, but the relationship was never consummated and now, in early February it is predicted to be sunny and 23 degrees C. I am sitting eating my boiled egg and toast on my balcony, with very good views, still inferior to those of the flat.

Nevertheless, I can see much that is the same. The flock of feral pigeons, whose nests in the few large pine trees are regularly raided by tree rats, still makes the morning discovery flight ensemble, before splitting later into twos (mostly twos now in early spring) and threes to while away the day before landing on the telegraph wires to make more musical notation. The kestrel, who sometimes adopts pigeon- like flight as a disguise, is in trembling mode, stationary on high, watching the field below for his morning feast. A few butterflies have begun to grace my garden, mostly what look like cabbage whites, but one tortoiseshell and some larger yellow ones whose name I am determined to know. It is too early for the invasion of the white Land Rovers, but they will be here soon, bearing their collection of visitors to admire the Sea Caves and chalk cliffs before bearing them off to the interior, on a day trip round the western part of the island.

The banana groves sit comfortably waving their fronds slightly in a sudden breeze. Each mature tree seems to have a new smaller one growing beneath it. I wonder if the management chops off the older one at some point? Well, I will be here to find out.

What will I do? Well for starters I have been writing this book. After that I have more stories that I want to write, I wake each morning with words and ideas going round in my brain, like a fizzling firework that I have to douse by tapping the computer keys before my head explodes. I hope it lasts.

Nick taught me to think that I might be loved by a man, despite my rather unprepossessing appearance. It altered my mindset, which is why I can now look happily over the balcony edge to see him busy gardening. He likes to "get into the garden" as he puts it, early in the day and then again in the evening, times when the sun is not too hot and watering and tending make most sense. He is learning and then teaching me and I seem to have fingers that are, if not actually green, at least greenery- yellary in that some of my seeds sprout and transplant successfully. This year we want to become self- sufficient in vegetables and salad crops.

 Nick sees me looking and waves. I return the wave and shout that I'll join him soon. Being pregnant has made me rather lazy. Life is good.

Printed in Great Britain
by Amazon

21395623R00210